"I THOUGHT PERHAPS YOU MIGHT LIKE TO WALK WITH ME IN THE GARDENS."

"I am afraid it is a trifle too cold for me, your lordship," Pip said, dismissing him with a distant smile.

Alex grasped her arm, pulling her gently but inexorably to her feet. "I insist, Miss Lambert."

The moment they were outside, she pulled free, her eyes snapping with fury. "I trust you know your behavior borders on the offensive?"

"And yours borders on the shrewish." Alex glared down into her angry face. The moonlight gave her skin a pearly gleam and turned her eyes into sparkling pools of forest green. His own anger gave way to the passion he had so long repressed, and unable to help himself, he lowered his head and took her mouth in a searing kiss . . .

D0660896

Other Regency Romances from Avon Books

By Kasey Michaels
THE CHAOTIC MISS CRISPINO
THE DUBIOUS MISS DALRYMPLE
THE HAUNTED MISS HAMPSHIRE
THE WAGERED MISS WINSLOW

By Loretta Chase
THE ENGLISH WITCH
ISABELLA
KNAVES' WAGER
THE SANDALWOOD PRINCESS
VISCOUNT VAGABOND

By Jo Beverley
EMILY AND THE DARK ANGEL
THE STANFORTH SECRETS

By Marlene Suson
DEVIL'S BARGAIN
THE FAIR IMPOSTOR

THE VISCOUNT'S VIXEN

JOAN OVERFIELD

AVON BOOKS ◆ NEW YORK

THE VISCOUNT'S VIXEN is an original publication of Avon Books. This work has never before appeared in book form. This work is a novel. Any similarity to actual persons or events is purely coincidental.

AVON BOOKS
A division of
The Hearst Corporation
1350 Avenue of the Americas
New York, New York 10019

First Avon Books Printing: November 1992

AVON TRADEMARK REG. U.S. PAT. OFF. AND IN OTHER COUNTRIES, MARCA REGISTRADA, HECHO EN U.S.A.

Printed in the U.S.A.

RA 10 9 8 7 6 5 4 3 2 1

To Kathie Hays
Because friends who are willing to loan you their computer are hard to find. My thanks once again.

THE VISCOUNT'S VIXEN

One

London, England 1815

"*Married!*" Miss Phillipa Lambert gasped, her green eyes wide as she leapt to her feet. "*You?* Please, Belle, tell me you are joking!"

Miss Arabelle Portham sat back in her striped chair, her face coolly composed as she returned her friend's incredulous gaze. "You must know I never joke," she returned in the distant manner which had earned her the title "The Golden Icicle." " 'Tis my intention to be married by Season's end, and I want your help to do it."

Pip could only shake her head, scarce believing the evidence of her own ears. She and Belle had been the best of friends for over seven years, and she would have sworn that she knew the icy blond better than anyone on earth. But this . . . she slowly lowered herself to her chair.

"Tell me again why you wish to marry," she said, smoothing the skirts of her prim gray gown and wondering if she ought to summon her aunt. As a rule, the elderly lady was a delightful widgeon with few thoughts in her head above the latest tidbits of gossip, but she was every bit as good as a physician when it came to diagnosing illnesses. Perhaps Belle only required a cup of beef tea to set her right again, Pip thought with growing hope.

"I think it was Miss Pettyforth's lecture that did it," Belle replied reflectively, raising her teacup to her lips. "You recall, Pip, it was the day we were going to Parliament to listen to the debates on the Corn Bill."

"I remember," Pip muttered, grimacing as she recalled the lecture her friend's newest companion had read them, reminding them in pious tones that a woman's position in society was rightfully determined by her husband. She then went on to hint broadly that so long as she and Belle pursued their "unfeminine" interest in politics, they would never get a man to wed them.

"Well, I have been thinking about what she said, and I have decided that she is right."

"What?" Pip started so violently that the tea in her cup sloshed over the gilded rim, burning her hand. She hastily set the cup back on its saucer and shot Belle an angry scowl.

"Now I know you are sickening after something," she accused, nursing her tender hand.

Rather than being offended, Belle was amused. "Thinking of having me bled, hm?" she asked, her amber-gold eyes bright with rare laughter. "Well, before you send for the leeches, I might remind you that while you may eschew matrimony, I do not share your dislike of the married state."

"And here I have always taken you for a female of superior intellect," Pip grumbled, her full mouth protruding in a pout. "Really, Belle, how can you be such a gudgeon? Marriage is but a sham designed to keep women in abject servitude, and one would have to be mad to willingly seek such a fate. It is as I have always said: 'Better the shroud—' "

" 'Than the veil.' " Belle finished the familiar remark, still smiling. "I know. But again, I do not share your misanthropy. Most females of our class do marry, and I am only doing what is expected of me."

"Perhaps," Pip conceded, cautiously picking up her teacup and partaking of a deep sip. "But most of them marry because they have no say in the matter, or because they foolishly fancy themselves to be in love. But you needn't bother with such fustian. You are wealthy, an heiress who has complete control of her own fortune. What can some pest of a man give you that you do not already have?"

"Power," Belle answered simply. "Political power."

Pip was quiet for a long moment. "But marriage won't grant you any power," she said at last, struggling to follow Belle's reasoning. "Women cannot vote. That is something that won't change even if you were to marry the king himself."

"That is so," Belle conceded with a gracious nod. "But what I *can* do is to become a political hostess. You must know that as an unmarried lady I can never hostess more than a small dinner party or an occasional musicale. My influence would be minimal at best. But as the wife of a politician . . ." Her voice trailed off enticingly.

"You could have unlimited influence," Pip concluded with a heavy sigh. Much as it galled her independent spirit to admit as much, she knew Belle's arguments were not without merit. As some man's wife, her friend would command far more power than she could ever achieve as a spinster—even a spinster who controlled a fortune of half a million pounds. Still . . .

"But if you married a politician, you would be expected to support his opinion," she protested, determined to dissuade the other woman from committing such a folly. "You might have more power, but that doesn't mean you would be free to use it. You would be naught but a reflection of him, and I can't see you settling for so meaningless an existence."

"Perhaps, but only if I married a man who *has* an opinion."

"What do you mean?"

Belle scooted closer to the edge of her chair. "What if I were to marry a young lord who is as indifferent to politics as we are fascinated by it?" she asked, her face glowing with eagerness. "Couldn't we then gently guide him along the correct path, perhaps even converting him to *our* way of thinking? He would vote the way we suggest, and at last we would have a voice in Parliament! Think about it, Pip!"

Pip thought about it. It made sense—in an awful sort of way, and she had to admit 'twas tempting. To actually have a say in the outcome of important political matters had long been a dream of hers. Why, it would almost be worth the bother of having some foolish man cluttering up one's parlor. In the next moment, however, she was shaking her head.

"No," she said firmly, "it would never work. Every man alive has opinions on something, and there is no guarantee you could convince him to vote the way you want him to."

"Not really. You know as well as I that 'tis not uncommon for over half the seats to remain unoccupied during session. Most of the members of the House of Lords don't give a fig how our country is governed, so long as their precious rights are protected! All we need to do is find some young lord who fits our needs, and then marry him. How difficult can it be? Come, Pip, what do you say? Will you help me?"

What the devil was he doing here? Lord Alexander St. Ives brooded, his dark face set with displeasure as he glanced about the crowded Assembly Room. He must have been bosky when he agreed to accompany Toby to Almack's—either that, or more bored than he dared admit. He had been in London for almost five weeks, and as far as he was concerned, 'twas time to go home.

"No need to look so Friday-faced, your lordship," the Honorable Tobias Flanders drawled in his affected manner, studying Marcus through his quizzing glass. "Surely things cannot be so wretched as all that!"

Alex quickly composed his expression, annoyed with himself for having allowed his feelings to be so evident that a cloth-head like Toby should take note of it. The other man was the younger cousin of one of his oldest friends, and he had promised Marcus he would keep an eye on him. What the earl had failed to tell him was that the young puppy was such an overweening dandy. A quick glance at his ornate cravat and multitude of fobs had Alex shuddering with fastidious displeasure.

"Nothing is wrong, Flanders," he answered in clipped tones, already weary of the younger man's presence. "I was merely thinking that it was time I was leaving."

"Leaving!" Toby stared at him with feigned horror. "I say, St. Ives, have you gone daft? The patronesses have yet to make their bows, and them old tabbies would cut up sharp was you to shab off now. 'Tis not done, old boy; not done at all."

The idea of Toby's taking him to task for a social solecism brought a glint of ironic laughter to Alex's dark blue eyes. "I wasn't referring merely to Almack's, Toby," he said, taking care to hide his amusement. "I was referring to the city. It is time I was returning to my estates."

"Quit London?" Judging from the dramatic way Toby clutched his chest, Alex could only presume he had deeply offended the dandy's sensibilities. "How can you even contemplate such a thing? London is the very center of our universe; how could you bear living anywhere else? 'Tis like that physician fellow said, "When a man is tired of London, he is tired of life!"

"Johnson."

"Eh?" Toby blinked his brown eyes in confusion.

"It is Dr. Samuel Johnson you are quoting," Alex explained, wondering why he was bothering. Toby was an idiot, and he couldn't imagine how he'd bumbled along this far. On the battlefield, he wouldn't have lasted an hour.

"As you say." Toby waved his hand vaguely. "My point, sir, is that there is naught that ails you save boredom. After defeating Boney I gather society is all rather flat, what?"

"Perhaps," Alex agreed, surprised by Toby's acuity. In truth, he *was* bored, and more than a little disgusted by the mindless way society pursued its pleasures. Oh, it had been amusing at first, and he'd enjoyed many of those pleasures himself. But lately when he looked in the mirror he didn't care for the reflection he saw looking back. It was time to go home and resume the duties he had set aside for a long-overdue holiday.

"Of course that is it." Toby looked smugly pleased with himself. "My late father once said the very same thing after returning from wherever it was he returned from. Said that after battle even lovemaking lacked a certain something. What you need, St. Ives, is a challenge, something to fire your imagination and your blood."

"My blood has already been sufficiently fired, thank you," Alex said, his mouth lifting in a very wolfish smile as he thought of his newest mistress. He would miss Althea and her skilled ways once he was back in Hampshire, although he knew better than to think she would want to accompany him. She was far too cosmopolitan to enjoy the country.

"I wasn't referring to fashionable impures." Toby sniffed, holding his quizzing glass to his eye, studying two ladies standing in the opposite corner. His mouth curled in a mocking smile. "Indeed," he continued in the same affected voice, "your success with our budding beauties is such that there is simply no sport in wagering on the potential outcome, was you to set out to win some doxy. The same is true of society's fairer flowers. But one cannot help but wonder how you would fare with a different sort of species . . . say, a ragweed?"

"What the devil are you talking about?"

"Well," Toby's tone fairly dripped with malice, "as I say, given your rank and fortune, there is no doubt you could conquer whatever chit you set your sights on. But if you was to take on a lady whose dislike of men was as well-known as her sharp tongue, then that would truly be a victory, would it not?"

"Again, Flanders, what the devil are you prattling on about?" Alex's patience was evaporating along with his control of his temper.

"That." Toby pointed the ivory handle of his quizzing glass at a tall brunette attired in an unfashionable gown of pale blue silk.

Alex stared at the woman. "Who is she?"

"Miss Phillipa Augusta Lambert, a lady of modest looks and fortune who is possessed of a sharp tongue and even sharper mind. She is, in fact, regarded as the worst bluestocking in London, and five hundred pounds says you can't win her!"

"Not *him!*" Pip exclaimed, studying with loathing the blond man across the room. "Have you lost your mind? Flanders is an out-and-out idiot! You'd be better off marrying one of the royals than that lack-witted, prattling fool!"

"Of course I wasn't referring to Flanders!" Belle retorted, her nose wrinkling in distaste. "I am not nearly so desperate as all that! I was speaking of the man next to him."

Pip's green eyes moved obligingly to the other man, noting with disinterest his black hair and handsome countenance. "Who is he?"

"Lord Alexander St. Ives, the new Viscount St. Ives," Belle provided, pleased with herself for having chosen so excellent a candidate. "He is newly arrived from the country, unmarried, and in the past five weeks, he has appeared at only four sessions. He is perfect, don't you think?"

"Mmm," Pip returned, her brows wrinkling. St.

Ives—the name rang a decided bell, and she struggled to make the connection. Then it came to her.

"St. Ives!" she cried, turning to look at Belle. "The man is worse than an idiot; he's a rake! He and Lord Colford all but had a duel over some doxy! Aunt said it was the talk of London for days. You couldn't possibly want to marry him!"

"Why not? It's not as if I love him, after all," Belle retorted, bristling over the mention of Lord Colford, whom she regarded as her own personal nemesis. "Besides, why should it matter to me whether or not he has a mistress? Let him take his pleasure where he will."

Pip found herself fighting a faint sense of shock. She liked to think of herself as an intellectual woman of the world, but there were times when Belle's cold practicality was more than a little disconcerting.

"Besides," Belle continued coolly, "the man also has a lovely country seat that is known for its hunting. Only think of the shooting parties we might stage! And everyone knows how politicians like to hunt."

"Yes, there is nothing like murdering scores of innocent deer and rabbits to turn a man up sweet," Pip retorted sourly, thinking that the more she considered this scheme of Belle's, the less she cared for it. It was one thing to agree when the whole thing was a nebulous plan, but quite another when the object of that plot was standing not twenty feet from her. Surely there was some way she could convince Belle to see the danger of her actions, she brooded, nervously chewing her bottom lip.

"That is so." Belle laughed, oblivious to Pip's concern. "But first things first; we must devise some scheme to meet him. I don't suppose Lady Jersey has forgiven you, and will introduce us to him?"

Pip shifted guiltily from one foot to the other as she recalled the patroness's displeasure at hearing a radical publication had printed one of her letters. "I still don't see how she found out," she muttered to hide her embarrassment. "I used a *nom de plume.*"

"Yes, 'Phillip Augustus'; very clever of you, I agree. But that doesn't answer my question. Do you think she will provide the necessary introductions?"

Pip considered the matter, weighing the older woman's annoyance with her against her fondness for matchmaking. "Perhaps," she said at last. "Especially if you were to simper and blush at the mention of the viscount's name. You must know there is nothing Old Sal likes better than prodding along a romance."

"Simper?" One of Belle's dark blond eyebrows arched over her eyes. "In all the years you have known me, have you ever known me to simper?"

"Well, no, but—"

"Good. Neither has Lady Jersey. If I were to start behaving like some silly Bath miss, she would know at once that I was up to something. How many times must I remind you not to be fooled by her ladyship's prattle? The old cat is sharper than the pair of us combined."

"A daunting prospect." Pip's green eyes danced with laughter. "Well, if you won't simper, then how do you propose we arrange matters? You must know she won't do it for *me.*"

"I don't know," Belle admitted, her golden eyes troubled. "But I shall think of something, never fear."

"Win her?" Alex regarded the young woman Toby had indicated with a worried frown. "Why the devil should I wish to win a bluestocking, of all things? Besides, Flanders, a gentleman would never bet on a young woman of breeding."

"Oh, posh." Toby tossed his head, causing the artfully arranged curls to tumble over his brow. "I don't mean you should bed her—"

"Toby, I warn you, if you say one more word . . ."

Toby sighed at the cold edge that appeared in Alex's voice. "You rakes are all alike. M'cousin's the same way. Wicked as the devil one minute, and then pokering up like a Methodist minister the next. Really, there is no understanding you."

"Good."

"What I *meant* to say is that you would win Miss Lambert's agreement to accompany you to some perfectly respectable social function—a ball, perhaps, or a play. That would be more than enough to prove your prowess."

"Rather flimsy proof, I should think," Alex said, although, of course, he had no intention of accepting the preposterous bet. He might be many things, but he wasn't so sunk he would bet against a young woman's good name. Even if she was a bluestocking, he added, noting Miss Lambert's bright-eyed expression with mild interest.

"That is because you ain't familiar with this particular lady," Toby said with a snicker. "The creature is as blue as a periwinkle, *and* a radical in the bargain. 'Tis said she even published an article in one of the more radical presses opposing the Corn Law."

"I see nothing so radical in that," Alex responded, although he frowned in slight disapproval.

"Perhaps not, but she was also heard to express the desire to vote; can you imagine? The only reason she ain't completely ostracized is because of her friendship with The Golden Icicle. There's few in society willing to cross half a million pounds, I can tell you."

"The what?" Alex could see the patronesses were lining up to receive their guests, and knew his torture was almost at an end. The moment he made his bows he would think of some emergency, and then make a discreet retreat.

"The blond statue standing next to her." Toby dutifully pointed out the other lady to Alex. "Worth a fortune, but you'd get more warmth from one of the Elgin Marbles."

"Are you discussing The Golden Icicle?" Reginald

Kingsford drifted over to join them. "Wouldn't bother if I was you. The lady may be rich as Croeseus, but she's far too sharp for my liking. Almost as bad as that Miss Lambert there."

"Precisely what I was telling Lord St. Ives." Toby bobbed his head in agreement. "In fact, I just wagered him a monkey he couldn't get her to accompany him to a ball."

Alex's eyes flashed with fire as he rounded on Toby. "Damn you, Flanders, I warned you," he began heatedly, only to be interrupted by the other man.

"A wager! I say, Flanders, that is infamous! Another five hundred that says he'll succeed."

Alex turned his displeasure on him. *"Gentlemen"*—he emphasized the word with cutting anger— "never wager on a lady. Period. You will forget this conversation ever took place, both of you."

"No bottom for deep play, eh?" Kingsford, the youngest of the three, looked disappointed. "Pity. I made sure you would win. A viscount and all, and handsome as Adonis. Even a bluestocking like Miss Lambert would be bound to accept your invitation."

The accusation of cowardice had Alex's fists clenching in fury. It was an accusation no gentleman could let stand—not if he valued his reputation in the clubs. For a moment, he felt like accepting, if only to silence the other man. Still, he hesitated, not wishing to involve an innocent lady in something with such potential for scandal.

"Bottom has nothing to do with this," he said, his voice tightly controlled. " 'Tis just that the terms are too uncertain for my liking. Having Miss Lambert accompany me to a ball hardly seems worth so much money, and since I refuse to do anything else which might compromise her good name, that is all there is to be said."

"Not necessarily," Toby corrected, tapping the handle of his quizzing glass against his cheek as he considered the matter. "I agree that bringing Miss Lambert to just any ball would not suffice, but there must be something, a special ball or some such which would provide sufficient proof. But . . ."

"The prince's ball at Carlton House!" the other man interrupted, all but clapping his hands in glee. "It is the perfect choice. Miss Lambert's disdain of the prince and his circle is well-known, and if she was to agree to accompany St. Ives there, it would be as good as a declaration!"

"Kingsford, how very practical of you!" Toby approved with a smile. "The prince's ball it shall be. Well, your lordship, what do you say?" He turned expectant brown eyes on Alex.

"I say you are both a pair of loonies, and I want no part of it," Alex responded through gritted teeth, making one last attempt to force them to see reason.

"Then you are refusing the wager?" Kingsford pressed, his thin mouth pursing in a smirk.

Alex roundly cursed him beneath his breath, admitting the little dandy had him. To refuse the bet would be tantamount to admitting defeat, and that was something he could not do. A gentleman's honor was a dicey thing, and he knew that once word got about to the clubs, he would be the laughingstock of London. Like it or not, there was nothing he could do but accept. His one hope was that word of the bet didn't spread beyond the three of them. For if it did, it would not be his name that suffered, but Miss Lambert's.

"Very well," he said heavily, "I accept, but with one proviso."

"And what is that?" Kingsford eyed him distrustfully.

"That neither of you tells a soul about this," Alex said, fixing them both in a steely blue glare. "This is among the three of us, and no one else. Agreed?"

"Well, if you do not think you will win," Kingsford began.

"Agreed?"

"Oh, very well." Toby gave a theatrical sigh. "Since you are going to be *that* way about it, I agree."

"Kingsford?" Alex turned to the younger man.

"As you wish, your lordship." He inclined his blond head mockingly. "I shan't tell another soul."

Alex gave him a hard look, wondering if he could believe him. There was something about his eyes he did not quite trust. "Very well, then, it is a bet," he said, glancing over to the corner to where Miss Lambert and the cool blond were standing, their heads together as if in earnest discussion.

At least the object of the bet was comely, he thought, his eyes lingering on the slender body displayed in the appalling gown. All that remained now was meeting her and convincing her to accompany him to the prince's ball. As Kingsford had said, he was a peer, and whatever airs Miss Lambert might choose to give herself, it was unlikely she would refuse an invitation from so eligible *un beau parti.* The bet was as good as won.

Two

"Introduce you to St. Ives?" Lady Jersey surveyed Pip with ill-disguised malice. "I should say not! The dear boy might be a Tory, but there are some things even *I* would not do to an enemy." And with a cutting smile she turned and stalked majestically away.

Pip watched her go, torn between amusement and chagrin. "I told you you should be the one to approach her," she said, flashing Belle a rueful smile. "It seems her ladyship hasn't quite forgiven me for my little indiscretion."

"Hinting that the Luddite riots are not without their merit is hardly a 'little' indiscretion," Belle replied, her slender brows gathering in a frown. "You're extremely lucky you weren't clapped into gaol over it."

"And so are you, considering you helped me draft it," Pip answered, scanning the room with narrowed eyes. "But I still fail to see why you are enacting a Cheltenham Tragedy over this. There are other patronesses, you know. I am sure Countess Lieven would be more than happy to perform the introductions, especially if she thought it would put Old Sal's nose out of joint. Or if worse comes to worst, you could push his lordship into the punch bowl. That has always been a time-honored way of attracting a gentleman's notice, or so I have heard."

Belle's lips twitched in an effort not to smile. "Brat,"

14

she accused without heat. "This is serious! The Season will be ending in a little over a month, and we shall have to step lively if we hope to fix his lordship's interest."

Lively indeed, if they hoped to wrangle a ring out of such a notorious rake, Pip thought, although she said nothing. Since Belle had fixed upon St. Ives, she had been recalling every single thing she had heard of the handsome viscount, and what she had heard was hardly reassuring. She'd rather see Belle married to a blustering tyrant like her father than shackled to a man who would surely disgrace his vows with every opera dancer and worldly widow who crossed his path.

As they always did, memories of her deceased father made her stomach tense with anger. Elias Lambert had been the worst sort of bully, using his cutting tongue and blazing temper to keep her and her timid mother firmly under his thumb. He had a low opinion of women, and he never let a day go by but that he didn't let Pip know he considered her a useless burden. The only reason he had left her his fortune was because there was no son to inherit, a blame he seemed more than willing to lay on her doorstep. As if it was somehow *her* fault she had been born a female, she brooded.

"I don't believe it!" Belle's fingers dug into Pip's arm, disrupting her reverie. "Lady Jersey is coming back!"

"If she's got a brigade of guardsmen with her, we'd best bolt for the border," Pip advised, shaking off her hurtful memories. "Despite what you may think, I've no desire to see the inside of a prison cell."

"No, there aren't any soldiers with her," Belle said in an odd tone of voice. "But she's not alone. Lord St. Ives is with her."

"What?" Pip whirled around, her jaw dropping as she watched a stiff-faced Lady Jersey threading her way through the crowds, the viscount striding boldly at her side. What on earth? she thought, and then the mismatched couple was standing before them.

"Miss Portham, Miss Lambert, how charming to see you again," Lady Jersey said, her stilted voice and wooden smile indicating she considered this meeting anything but charming. "You are enjoying yourselves, I trust?"

"Indeed, your ladyship," Belle responded with a serene smile. "In fact, Miss Lambert and I were just commenting on how delightful everything is. Weren't we?" She shot Pip a meaningful look.

"Utterly delightful," Pip agreed obligingly, thinking that while Belle might draw the line at simpering, she obviously saw nothing wrong with a bit of judicious toadying.

"How nice." Having dispensed with the niceties, the countess turned to the viscount, who had been standing quietly beside her. "Ladies, I do not believe you are acquainted with Lord St. Ives. He arrived in the city a few weeks ago."

"No, we have not yet met." Belle held out a slender hand, dropping a graceful curtsey as Lady Jersey performed the necessary introductions.

"Miss Portham, allow me to present you to Lord Alexander St. Ives. Your lordship, Miss Arabelle Portham."

"Your lordship."

"Miss Portham."

The two exchanged civil greetings, and then Lady Jersey's light blue eyes came to rest on Pip. "And this is Miss Phillipa Lambert, one of our more learned ladies. Miss Lambert, Viscount St. Ives."

"Your lordship." Pip also curtsied, her eyes demurely downcast as she sought to hide her amusement. She didn't doubt but that it must be choking the countess to perform the small, social task, and she couldn't help but wonder what incentive the viscount had brought to bear to force the introduction. She was fairly certain the meeting wasn't any of Lady Jersey's doing.

"Miss Lambert." Alex bowed over her hand, thinking that so far everything was going just as he had planned. When he'd seen the countess speaking to Miss Lambert and the pretty blond, he'd decided to request an introduction, and was surprised when she'd curtly refused. It had taken a great deal of persuasion on his part, but at last the older lady had grudgingly relented, muttering dire warnings beneath her breath as they made their way through the press of the crowd.

"Don't let that dowdy air fool you for one moment, sir. The creature is a hellcat and a minx. Writing *tracts,* if you will, and having them printed in some wretched journal. If she were a man, she'd be in Botany Bay by now, and good riddance I should say! No title and less than a thousand pounds *per annum;* hardly worth society's attention. Can't think why we keep letting her in."

He had not deigned to reply, although his curiosity was piqued. Glancing at the slender brunette, he found it hard to imagine how she had so successfully alienated so many influential people. Again he felt a stab of guilt for having accepted the bet, an emotion he hid behind his most winning smile.

"It is a pleasure to meet you, Miss Lambert. May I request the next dance? Unless, of course, you have promised it to another?"

His request brought Pip's head jerking up in disbelief. She'd assumed he'd requested the introduction to meet Belle, not her. "But I don't dance," she blurted out, her eyes going to Belle as she sought advice.

"Nonsense." Alex retained her hand, determined to get all this behind him as quickly as possible. "I am sure Lady Jersey has no objections to our dancing. Have you, your ladyship?" His cold blue eyes flicked in the countess's direction.

"Certainly not," Lady Jersey replied quickly, relieved

at having performed the requested duty. She didn't know why such a handsome and eligible man as St. Ives should be dangling after a quiz like Miss Lambert, but she meant to find out.

"Now if you children will excuse me, I really must be going. I see Lady Cowper speaking with Lady Bessville, and I must go rescue her. Goodbye."

There was an awkward silence, and then Pip turned to Alex. "You will note she did not say who it was who required rescuing," she said with a smile. "And as for yourself, your lordship, you may also consider yourself safely rescued."

"Rescued?" Alex raised a dark eyebrow.

"There is no reason for you to dance with me," she explained, as if to a child. "I am a wretched dancer and would most certainly make a cake of myself. Belle, however, is most accomplished, aren't you, darling?" She gave Belle an encouraging smile.

Before the other woman could reply, Alex took Miss Lambert's arm in a firm hold. "You must not put Miss Portham to the blush, ma'am," he said in a voice that was both teasing and firm. "And if I may refresh your memory, it was you Lady Jersey gave me permission to escort on the dance floor, not Miss Portham. We wouldn't wish to place her in an untenable position."

A lecture on propriety from a rake? Pip was sadly disappointed. She would have preferred the viscount to be a trifle more of an iconoclast and less of a prig. She was about to make her refusal more obvious when the first strains of the waltz reached her ears. Realizing she was trapped, she allowed the viscount to lead her out on to the dance floor.

They had made three successful rotations about the room when Alex said, "You have played me false, Miss Lambert. You dance with the grace of a zephyr."

"And you, sir, lie with the skill of a seasoned politician," Pip responded, mentally wincing as she brought her slippered foot down on his. "If you would like to beg off, I shall certainly understand."

"What a poor opinion you have of me, ma'am, to think I would quit the field before the battle is scarce joined. I am not so easily frightened."

His choice of words struck Pip as amusing. "So it is to be war, then?" she asked, feeling greatly daring. She'd never tried flirting before, and decided the sensation was oddly exhilarating.

"Is it not always war between a man and a woman?" Alex replied smoothly. Miss Lambert was proving to be far more biddable than he had thought, and he was amazed to find he was a trifle disappointed. He'd been rather anticipating taming a shrew. As it was now, he did not doubt but that he would prove successful. A few more flattering words on her dancing ability, and then he would invite her to the prince's ball. How could she refuse?

"Or a political debate," she agreed, deciding she'd had enough of playing coy. She was enjoying the waltz far more than she cared to admit, but it was time she kept her promise to Belle. The first step was to learn just for herself how he felt about political issues. She tilted her head back and gave him a look that was deliberately provoking. "Not that you would know about such things, of course."

Her mocking words brought Alex's foot down on the toe of her slipper. After an embarrassed apology, he gave her a confused look. "What did you mean by that?"

"Nothing." She gave him a superior smile. "The music is lovely, is it not?"

Alex ignored her, concentrating instead on her earlier remark. When the dance ended he escorted her off the floor, leading her to a private corner so that he could continue their conversation. He was hanged if he would allow her oblique comment to pass unremarked.

"I happen to be well-acquainted with political debate, Miss Lambert," he informed her in icy tones, his pursed lips and clenched jaw mute evidence of his displeasure. "I am a member of the House of Lords, you know."

"And haven't made it to more than a handful of sessions," she agreed, delighted at having incurred his displeasure. She would have to warn Belle of his pompous temper, she thought, with a hidden smile. Evidently the viscount took himself more seriously than they had first supposed.

This hint that he had neglected his duty brought a dangerous glitter to Alex's eyes. All his life he had put duty before all else, and her accusation flicked him raw on his pride. "I may not have been as devoted in my attendance as some," he admitted in a voice that would have made many a man back away, "but never doubt for a moment that I am not fully aware of my responsibilities."

"Then why did you miss the debate on Monday?" she pressed, with that same maddening smile. "You must know they are getting ready to vote on the proposed changes in the Corn Bill. The debate was crucial to the outcome of that act."

"The debate was on Monday?" he demanded in a low, furious voice. "It wasn't supposed to take place until tomorrow!"

"Ah, but you know how you Tories are," Pip drawled mockingly. "Always one step ahead of the game. And of course there was the fact the number of Tories greatly outnumber the few Whigs in attendance. Although I am sure that was only a happy coincidence."

"Blast it, I was supposed to give a speech," he muttered, the matter of the bet slipping his mind in the light of this latest development. "And to think I did nothing that day but visit my tailor," he added, more to himself than her. Unfortunately she heard, and was quick to make use of it.

"Duty to one's tailor must, of course, take preference over duty to one's country," she agreed derisively. "I understand. I only hope your fellow Tories share your sartorial sentiments. That way we Whigs shan't have any trouble defeating this ruinous bill."

Her bold declaration brought Alex's dark brows snapping together. "I had heard you were an impertinent bluestocking," he said cuttingly, deciding no bet was worth tolerating such abuse.

"And I had heard you were naught but a care-for-nothing rake," she returned in kind, still delighted. "How refreshing it is to know one may rely on the veracity of society's tattle, *n'est-ce pas?*"

"You—" For a moment Alex feared losing his temper and any claim to being a gentleman. It took a great deal of effort, but he at last gained enough control over himself to speak. "I believe it is time I returned you to Miss Portham," he said in a voice as cold as a wind off a January sea. "I am sure she must be wondering what happened to you."

"I am sure she must," Pip agreed, her amusement vanishing at the suppressed fury in his deep voice. To be sure, she'd enjoyed twitting the wretch, but she certainly hadn't meant to alienate him, as she greatly feared she had. Wonderful, she thought, as a silent St. Ives escorted her to the corner where her Aunt Morwenna and Belle were waiting. Not only was the viscount a rake and a Tory, but it also appeared he hadn't one iota of a sense of humor. Clearly she and Belle would have to rethink the situation.

The crowds at Almack's and her aunt's presence prevented Pip from filling Belle in on what had transpired. It wasn't until early the following afternoon, when Belle stopped by for a cup of tea, that she was finally able to give a full report. As she'd expected, Belle was far from pleased.

"Forget St. Ives?" she repeated, once she finished

speaking. "But Pip, whatever can you mean? I have told you, the viscount is perfect for our needs!"

"A perfect prig is what you mean," Pip muttered, green eyes bright as she raised her tea cup to her lips. "The man is a pompous, overbearing tyrant, and you may take it from me that the last thing he would ever tolerate is to be guided by anyone, especially a woman!"

"So?" Belle gave an indifferent shrug. "The same might be said of any man. I can hardly disqualify his lordship on that basis alone, else I would have to rule out every other man in England as well. The trick with men, my dear, is to guide them in such a way that they are unaware as to what is happening."

"Easier said than done," Pip retorted, remembering St. Ives's cold anger as he spoke of fulfilling his responsibilities. "For all we took him for a fashionable fribble, the man is hardly a fool. You would have better luck in taming a tiger than making a complaisant husband out of that wretch."

Belle set her cup down with a clatter. "I wasn't aware I regarded St. Ives as a 'fribble,' " she said, every inch The Golden Icicle. "Indeed, I would want nothing to do with such a creature. I may desire a *mariage de convenance,* but that doesn't mean I would settle for just anybody! If nothing else, I would wish to have some modicum of respect for my husband."

"Perhaps," Pip conceded, determined to convince Belle to see the error of her ways, "but I still say we have committed a grave error in judgement. You said you wished a man who had no real opinion, and St. Ives not only has opinions, but he is fully prepared to air them in front of Parliament!"

Belle picked up her teacup, her brief flare of temper forgotten as she mulled over Pip's accusations. "True," she said at last, her tone thoughtful, "but I have been thinking, and I have decided that it may not necessarily be a bad thing. It wouldn't do for my husband to be *completely* indifferent to politics."

Pip opened her mouth to object and then fell silent. "I suppose you are right," she admitted, albeit with the greatest reluctance. "Not that it signifies one way or another. Judging from the way his lordship stalked off in high dudgeon last night, I much doubt we shall be seeing him again."

"Yes, it was unfortunate the two of you came to daggers so quickly," Belle replied, tilting her head to one side as she regarded Pip. "Whatever could you have said to cast him up into the boughs like that?"

"What *I* said?" Pip bristled at the injustice of her friend's accusation. "What about what he said? The man called me an impertinent bluestocking!"

"You *are* an impertinent bluestocking."

"Perhaps, but that doesn't mean I welcome having the fact thrown in my teeth!" Pip ignored the teasing tone in her friend's voice. "And what is more, the man is a complete rake! Until we began discussing politics, he was flirting with me like the very devil. He was as full of butter as a piece of pastry, all smiles and sweet words as he complimented me on my atrocious dancing. He would have been kissing my hand next, and composing odes to my green eyes!"

"I like pastry." Dimples flashed in Belle's cheeks as she smiled up at Pip.

Pip glared at her a full moment, and then raised her eyes heavenward as she realized nothing she had said had dissuaded her friend in the least. "Has anyone ever told you that you can be most annoyingly obstinate?" she asked, sighing resignedly.

Belle's golden eyes lost their smile. "One man," she said coolly. "But as he is one of those overbearing tyrants you so dislike, we shan't waste our time discussing him."

That struck Pip as most intriguing, but before she could demand an explanation there was a knock on the door and her aunt, Mrs. Morwenna Beachton, came scurrying in the room.

"My apologies for disturbing you, dear Phillipa," she said, her thin hands clasped in front of her, "but you did say you wished to go to Parliament in order to hear the afternoon debates, and it is already gone past two."

Pip's eyes stole at once to the gilded clock adorning the marble fireplace. "It cannot be so late as that!" she cried, the viscount forgotten as she surged to her feet. "Oh dear, Belle, we had best hurry or we shall be most shockingly late."

A rare smile lit Belle's lovely features as she too rose to her feet. "I would not worry if I were you," she said in an ironic tone of voice. "Considering how slow the House moves, they will still be droning on come midnight. It is doubtful we shall miss anything of import regardless of when we arrive."

There she was. Alex smiled coldly at the sight of Miss Lambert and Miss Portham making their way toward the front of the hall. Miss Lambert was dressed in an unfashionable pelisse of brown velvet, a no-nonsense bonnet perched on her dark curls. He wondered for a moment why she should choose to dress like a poor relation when by all indications her pockets were deep enough to allow her to deck herself out in the height of fashion, and then shrugged his shoulders in disinterest. It was really no concern of his; all that mattered was that he have his chance for a second go at her.

When he'd stormed out of Almack's last night he'd been so coldly furious with her that he'd have willingly forfeited the wager on the spot. She was an opinionated, ill-mannered hoyden, and he'd rather have lost five *thousand* pounds than ever go within an inch of her again. How dare the little shrew presume to pass judgement on him and then find him wanting?

It was this thought that had kept him awake most of the night, and the more he considered her insults the angrier he became. He'd fallen into an uneasy sleep, only to awaken filled with a sense of purpose he hadn't known since resigning his commission. Loath as he had originally been to enter into the wager, he now found he was committed to carrying out his end of the bet. This was personal, he admitted grimly, and although he would still do his best to protect the lady's name, he was resolved to emerge the victor of their contest. No one else would ever know, but at least he would have the satisfaction of knowing he had bested her. All that remained now was to regain whatever ground he had lost last night.

Wellington had taught him to use an enemy's weaknesses against him, and as he already knew her greatest weakness to be politics, he'd laid his plans accordingly. Surmising that she would be unable to resist attending the debating session, he'd cancelled his standing appointment at Gentleman Jackson's Salon and presented himself at Parliament in time for the opening debates. He was beginning to think he had missed her entirely when he'd caught a glimpse of her and Miss Portham, accompanied by Mrs. Beachton, descending the visitor's staircase. Murmuring an apology to a colleague who was attempting to detain him, he pushed forward until he was standing between her and the doorway. He had only to step back and—

"Oh! Excuse me, sir!" Pip's apology was automatic as she collided with the tall, broad-shouldered man who seemed to have appeared out of nowhere. "I trust I did not . . . Lord St. Ives!"

"Miss Lambert!" The surprise on Alex's face as he glanced from Pip's stunned face to those of her companions would have done the great Edmund Kean proud. "How delightful to see you! I looked for you earlier in the visitor's gallery, but did not see you."

"We were a trifle late in arriving," Pip responded,

more than a little surprised by the friendliness of his greeting. Considering the acrimonious way they had parted, she wouldn't have been the least bit shocked had he cut her dead on the spot. What was going on here? she wondered, studying him through narrowed eyes.

"Ah, then you missed my speech." He pretended to be hurt, his dark blue eyes reproachful. "I did tell you, did I not, Miss Lambert, that I had composed one?"

"Indeed you did, your lordship," she answered, still wary. "But it was my understanding that you had . . . er . . . missed your opportunity to give it? Something about a pressing appointment, if I recollect correctly."

" 'Pressing appointment,' very clever, Miss Lambert." He gave a self-deprecatory laugh before turning to the other ladies. "I missed the last session to keep an appointment with my tailor," he said, including them in his guileless smile. "And Miss Lambert was quick to take me to task for my shocking dereliction."

"I beg your pardon, your lordship, but I did not take you to task," Pip denied, blushing at his words. In the face of his good-natured admission she felt like the greatest humbug alive, and she wondered if perhaps she had been a trifle hasty in her judgement. Her father, for example, would never have been so amiable about such a thing.

"Rang a blistering peal over my head and accused me of abetting the enemy—the Whigs, that is, and not the blasted French," he continued in the same easy tones. "I own I was mad as the devil at first, but now I have decided I am grateful for her sharp tongue."

"Grateful?" Belle raised her eyebrow at him before casting a speaking glance in Belle's direction. "How so, sir?"

"Because she reminded me of my duty," Alex responded. "I have been neglecting it, you see."

"I am sure my niece meant nothing of the sort, Lord St. Ives," Mrs. Beachton said, her brown eyes censorious as they rested on Pip. "One has only to look at your war record to know that such is not the case."

"War record?" Pip and Belle echoed the words in unison.

"A few skirmishes, nothing of import," Alex said with a modesty that was not wholly faked. Proud as he was of his years in the Rifles, he wasn't one of those men who enjoyed wrapping themselves in the glory of heroism, and not even for the sake of the wretched wager would he reveal the details of his service.

"Nonsense." Mrs. Beachton was not so sensitive as to pick up on his obvious hint. "Don't let the lad fool you. He held the rank of major, fought in a dozen different battles, and was mentioned in several dispatches. There were even a few citations for bravery under fire, as I recall."

Belle and Pip exchanged sick looks. "I see." Pip was the first to recover the ability to speak, and she was sunk with shame to think she had dismissed him so lightly. Looking at him now, his blue eyes earnest and his tanned jaw set with determination, she wondered how she could have been so misguided. Evidently her powers of observation were not so developed as she would like to believe, she decided with a flash of rueful humor.

"I am sorry we missed your speech, your lordship," Belle offered with a polite smile. "Might I ask you what it contained? Do you support or oppose the changes?"

"A little of both, actually. I can see the need to protect the interests of our farmers even as I see the necessity for cheap bread for our poor," Alex responded dutifully, annoyed by the interruption. Miss Lambert was his objective, and he disliked being diverted by anything, even a wealthy beauty like Miss Portham.

"Ah, so there is hope for you yet," Belle replied with a pleased nod. "Good. Pip would have it that you were a dyed-in-the-wool Tory beyond redemption."

Pip's jaw dropped at this out-and-out fabrication. "I never said—"

"There is to be a meeting on the subject at Mayfield Gardens tomorrow," Belle continued, not paying Pip the slightest mind. "As it is open to the public, we ladies are being admitted. Will you also be attending?"

Alex's smile slipped a notch. He had heard about the proposed meeting, and from what he had heard, it was expected to degenerate into a riot like those that had convulsed the city in February. Feelings on the Corn Bill ran high, especially in the area of town where the meeting was to be held, and he could not like the thought of Miss Lambert and her friend being exposed to the dangers of a London mob. He was about to forbid them from attending at all when common sense stilled his tongue.

"I had been considering it, yes," he said guardedly, watching them through narrowed eyes. "And what of you ladies? Do I take it you will be attending?"

"We had been considering it," Pip echoed ironically, noting the speculative look that flashed across his face. Now that she'd learned more of him, she was less willing to accept his every word without question. Something was definitely afoot here, and she wondered what that something was.

"Then you must allow me to act as your escort," Alex interjected smoothly, pleased at how easily he had turned the situation to his advantage. "That is not a very safe section of town, and it would not be advisable for you ladies to venture there without proper escort. Naturally we shall take my carriage."

Such condescension was more than Pip's pride could tolerate. While she was more than willing to admit she may have misjudged him, that did not mean she would allow him to dictate her behavior. Eyes flashing with indignation, she was about to administer a sharp setdown when Belle astounded her by saying:

"That is very gracious of you, your lordship. At what time shall we expect you?"

Again Miss Portham's interference annoyed Alex, although this time he was grateful for it. If he was any judge of Miss Lambert, she had been about to hurl his offer back in his face, and Miss Portham's acceptance had forestalled her. "The meeting is to begin at one o'clock," he said, addressing his answer to her. "Shall we say twelve thirty?"

"But I wished to get there early," Pip protested, glowering at both Lord St. Ives and her traitorous friend. "If we don't leave until then, all the good places will be gone before we arrive!"

Good, Alex thought, thinking that if things turned ugly he wanted to be as far from the mob as possible. "That is a risk we shall have to take," he replied, taking care to keep his voice as pleasant as possible. "You live in Belgravia, I believe?"

"On Wilton Place," Pip provided, accepting his presence with a resigned sigh. "Number four."

"Then I shall see you there," he said, toying with the notion of kissing her hand. But he discarded the idea as unwise. Judging from the sour looks she was casting at him, he'd already aroused her suspicions, and he didn't wish to destroy everything he had achieved by rushing his fences.

Patience, he cautioned himself as he took his leave of the ladies with a formal bow, patience. The trait had served him well on the battlefield, and it would serve him well now. In one week, perhaps two, he would have his victory. He savored the thought with a wolfish smile.

Three

Pip waited until they'd reached Belle's carriage before giving vent to her annoyance. " 'I never simper,' " she quoted, throwing herself against the thick leather squabs and casting a fulminating glare at Belle. "Ha! You could have put the greenest deb to the blush with your antics! Really, Belle, have you no shame?"

"When it comes to getting what I wish, no," Belle answered with blunt honesty, calmly untying the ribbons of her elegant bonnet. "And you needn't look so outraged, either. You have read enough Machiavelli to know that politics is the art of persuasion."

"Persuasion is one thing; comporting oneself like a desperate spinster at her last prayers is another," Pip grumbled, burning at the eager way Belle had accepted St. Ives's offer rather than boxing his ears as she ought to have done.

"Phillipa, you shouldn't take that tone with Belle." Mrs. Beachton bestirred herself enough to offer her niece a gentle setdown. "And although I do not know this Macaroni fellow she is quoting, I must say he has the right of it. Sugar draws far more flies than vinegar, you know."

"Yes, Aunt," Pip answered, thinking that "fly" was a very apt description for St. Ives. The man was proving to be as annoying as any insect, and there was no doubt in her mind but that he wasn't buzzing after something.

"I must say I am vexed to hear St. Ives was in the army." Belle had removed her bonnet and was staring out the window, a pensive expression on her face. "From what I had learned of him, I took him to be little more than a dilettante lord."

"Heavens, no!" Mrs. Beachton exclaimed, clearly shocked. "He was in my late husband's regiment, and I remember Harry oft mentioned his lordship's dedication to his duty. Of course," she added reflectively, "that was when he was just plain Major Daltry of the Rifles, long before he inherited his title, but I cannot imagine he has changed so completely. Leopards don't change their spots, as dear Harry was forever telling me."

Accustomed as she was to her aunt's propensity to quote her deceased husband at the slightest provocation, Pip didn't reply. In the five years since the older woman had come to live with her, she had heard the general's opinion quoted so many times she felt as if the old windbag was still alive. Still, something her aunt said puzzled her, and she turned to her with a frown.

"Then St. Ives has only recently come into the title?" she asked, her brows pleating in thought.

"Not quite two years, if memory serves," Mrs. Beachton provided obligingly. "I recall seeing the notice of Edmund's death and thinking what a double tragedy it was. First poor Roderick gets himself killed in that curricle race, then Edmund succumbs to the fever not six months later. Too tragic by half, if you ask me."

Pip sifted through the mountain of information her aunt had let fall. "Who is Roderick?" she asked, struggling to make sense of the Homeric saga.

"Well, nobody now!" Her aunt gave her an annoyed frown. "I just told you, the wretch broke his neck in a curricle race."

"Then who *was* he?" Pip made a grab at patience. "St. Ives's brother?"

"His uncle. A neck-or-nothing Corinthian who was scarce in his forties when he died. He was a bachelor, and as there was no heir, the title passed to Edmund, who promptly proved his ingratitude by catching cold and dying of the fever. He was St. Ives's elder brother by two years, I believe."

That her aunt should be so intimately acquainted with the details of St. Ives's life came as no real surprise to Pip. The older woman was forever studying Debrett's Peerage and exchanging information with her cronies, elderly ladies like herself who busied themselves sniffing out even the smallest scrap of gossip about the *ton*. Pip doubted there was anything of import that escaped their notice, and the notion appealed to her wry sense of humor. Wellington may have prided himself on his intelligence network, she thought, but he was a babe in arms compared to the ladies of her aunt's acquaintance.

"I knew about the deaths of his uncle and brother, of course," Belle was saying, her golden eyes troubled. "But I neglected to check beyond that. A serious error in calculation, it would appear."

Pip brightened at the uncertainty in her friend's voice. "Then perhaps we can remove his lordship's name from consideration," she said hopefully. After this latest encounter with the viscount, she was more convinced than ever that he and Belle would not suit. There was something about him she could not trust.

"I think we need not be so hasty as all that," Belle answered, indicating Pip's aunt with a subtle jerk of her head. "In the meanwhile, I am grateful his lordship has consented to escort us to Mayfield's. It was very generous, do you not think so, ma'am?" She turned a singularly sweet smile on Mrs. Beachton.

"Very generous," the older woman agreed, nodding her turbaned head in approval. "Although I do not see why the pair of you should ever want to attend such a thing. Political meetings! I vow, I can not think what this world is coming to. Young ladies never bothered with such things in *my* day, I can tell you."

Neither Belle nor Pip responded, having learned the futility of defending their position. While Belle accepted such censure with a philosophical shrug, Pip was less sanguine, and her proud spirit chafed at the restrictions placed upon her. As a small child, she'd had no choice but to bow to her bullying father, but now that she was a grown woman she was determined to follow her own mind. No man would ever tell her what to do or how to think, she vowed with a proud lift of her chin. And that went double for arrogant lords with brooding midnight-blue eyes, and a face too coldly handsome to be trusted.

"What do you mean you aren't going?" Pip wailed, staring at Belle's supine form with dismay. "Blast it, Belle, you have to go! This is all your idea!"

Belle winced at the sound of Pip's voice and raised a shaking hand to her head. "Please," she begged in a whisper, "not so loud, I implore you. My head feels as if it will fall off."

"I'm sorry." Pip capitulated at once. She knew Belle to be plagued by occasional migraines, but this was the first time she could recall seeing her friend cast so low. She eyed Belle's pale features and nibbled worriedly at her bottom lip. "Do you think we ought to send for a doctor?"

Belle shook her head, then moaned at the pain. "He would only prescribe laudanum, and I would as lief suffer as take that devil's brew. I will be all right on the morrow."

Pip fell into an uncomfortable silence, not knowing what else to say. When Belle's note had been delivered scarce an hour ago, Pip had come tearing over to Belle's house determined to do whatever it took to insure that she kept their appointment with St. Ives. But glancing at her friend now, Pip knew she couldn't press

the issue. Whatever her other faults, Belle was no ma-
lingerer, and Pip could only imagine the pain her poor
friend must be suffering to prevent her from keeping
her word.

"Well, all is not lost," Pip said in comforting tones.
"It is hours yet before St. Ives is due to meet us, and
I can easily write him a note of apology explaining the
situation to him."

That brought one of Belle's pain-filled eyes flying
open, if only briefly. "But I want you to go," she said
weakly. "This is the perfect opportunity for you to observe his lordship at close quarters."

"Too close. You must know I cannot possibly accompany him in a carriage without a chaperone of some
sort," Pip reminded her, grateful for once for the chains
society placed upon unmarried females.

"Your aunt . . ."

". . . is at the Royal Society for Widows of the
Guard," Pip finished for her. "And I doubt a maid
would be considered sufficient protection in this case."

Belle was silent for a long moment. "You are right,
of course," she said with a heavy sigh. "Still, I can not
help but be sorry. Lord St. Ives hardly travels in our circles, and who knows when we may get another opportunity like this one."

This was the opportunity Pip had been waiting for.
For a moment she was strongly tempted to renew her
arguments concerning St. Ives's ineligibility. But another glance at Belle's face silenced her, and she rose
reluctantly to her feet.

"I will write the letter at once," she promised, laying
a soothing hand on Belle's arm. "You just rest. When I
come to see you tomorrow, I shall give you a full report
of the meeting. They say Leigh Hunt himself may be
addressing the gathering."

Belle's eyes fluttered open. "But you cannot mean to
go alone," she protested in a wan voice. "I have been
thinking, and much as I hate to say it, I fear St. Ives is

right. That part of London is hardly the safest of places, especially given the current mood of the people. I think it may be wisest if you did not go."

Despite her empathy for her friend's suffering, Pip could not help but bristle. "Nonsense," she said in her sternest voice. "The older part of the city is far safer than some of the area where you go in search of your good works. I shall be perfectly safe, I promise you."

"But—"

"No, no, my mind is quite made up," Pip interrupted, unbending enough to deposit a loving kiss on Belle's cheek. "I'll stand meekly in the farthest corner of the crowd and not say boo to a goose. It will be fine; you'll see."

"I say, St. Ives, if this is your idea of a good time then I fear you are an even duller stick than I first thought," Tobias drawled, executing a distasteful shudder as he studied the ragged mob pressing against the wheels of the viscount's hired carriage. "This ain't any place for a gentleman of fashion."

"Shut up, Flanders," Alex replied, searching the teeming crowd for any sign of Miss Lambert. When the note cancelling their engagement had arrived, he'd been both relieved and annoyed. He had no real desire to attend a meeting of revolutionaries, but on the other hand, he had welcomed the chance to ensnare his prey in his net. Arriving at her home on the off chance she might agree to accompany him on a brief ride, he'd been horrified to learn she had set off to the meeting alone, without even a footman or a maid to protect her. Although why he should be surprised he knew not; the woman was clearly a shrew with little if any regard for the proprieties.

"No need to take m'head off." Toby sniffed, clearly taking issue with Alex's snarled command. "I am worried about you. You was a right jolly fellow until you waltzed with that she-devil. Now look at you, making speeches and attending political meetings! You'll start powdering your hair and sermonizing next, I don't wonder."

"You are free to leave if you don't care for the company," Alex responded, his eyes narrowing as the crowd momentarily parted, giving him a glimpse of a tall woman in a brown pelisse.

" 'Tis not that, 'tis just ... what the devil are you doing?"

"Stay here until I get back, if you can," Alex said, opening the door and stepping out. "But if things turn ugly, I want you to get the devil out of here. I can always hire another hack."

"What? What?" Toby repeated, clearly horrified. "I say, St. Ives, where the deuce are you going? You can't leave me here!" But St. Ives was already gone, swallowed up by the surging crowd.

It had taken Pip less than five minutes to realize she had made a mistake in coming. Rather than the civilized debate she had been expecting, the meeting was rapidly deteriorating into a brawl, and she greatly feared things would only get worse. All around her people were screaming and shouting, shaking their fists and calling for the downfall of the government. She was being pushed and pulled from a dozen different directions, and more than once she found herself fighting to keep her footing.

"To devil with yer talk!" a thin man standing to Pip's left suddenly shouted. "Enough o' talk; I say we act! To the king! To the king! He won't let us starve!"

"Aye! To the king!" a second voice sounded. " 'e'll make them leeches in Parliament give us what's rightly ours!"

"To hell with kings!" Another voice came from Pip's right. "Death to 'em all! Bread, not royalty!"

In a twinkling the shout became a rallying cry, and before Pip's horrified eyes the crowd became a mob, moving with no thought or logic to guide it. People began shoving one another as if in a frenzy, and several people were knocked to the ground. One particularly strong shove sent her staggering, and she fell beneath the feet of the mob. Just as she was certain she would be trampled, a strong arm closed about her waist and hauled her unceremoniously to her feet.

"Stay with me, damn it," St. Ives shouted urgently in her ear, "or I swear to heaven I shall leave you here to deal with your own folly!" And before Pip could answer him, he began fighting his way out of the frenzied crush of people.

"Wait!" Pip protested, struggling to keep pace with his longer strides. "Not so fast, I can't . . . look out!" She screamed sharply as a large man wielding a club interposed himself between St. Ives and the far end of the field.

St. Ives took the man down with a swift kick to the stomach, and continued pulling Pip along behind him. Several of the man's friends cried out in protest, their voices blending with the cacophony of other cries. Pip could feel hands snatching at her, but St. Ives held on to her with remarkable strength. Finally they reached the outer edge of the horde, and the sight of St. Ives's hired hack brought a sob of relief to Pip's lips. St. Ives tore open the door and tossed her inside, throwing himself protectively over her as he called out a loud command.

"Get us the hell out of here!"

The driver needed no second warning. He cracked his whip over the heads of the nervous horses, and they were off with a lurch. Shouts could still be heard through the heavy wooden doors, and when a rock came smashing through the window, it was all Pip could do not to scream again.

Finally they were out of the mob, and Alex warily raised himself, glaring down at Miss Lambert with a mixture of annoyance and concern. "Are you all right?"

he demanded, studying her for any sign of injury. "Did anyone hurt you?"

"No, I am f–fine, thank you," Pip replied, struggling to regain control over her badly-shattered senses. She was well aware of how close she had come to being seriously injured, and the knowledge left her shaking in reaction.

Alex felt the tremor that shook her body, and it brought to mind the unseemliness of their current situation. Cursing beneath his breath, he rose to a sitting position, lifting her onto the bench opposite him at the same time.

"Are you quite certain you are all right?" he pressed, his brows gathering in a worried frown at the pallor of her dirt-streaked face. "We can send for a physician if—"

"No!" Pip interrupted, regaining her composure with each passing second. "I told you, I am uninjured. It is just I . . . I have never seen anything like that before. Was anyone hurt, do you think?" She gave him an anxious look.

"I'm not certain," Alex lied, leaving out the fact that he'd seen more than one or two ominously still forms lying on the muddied ground. "But if they were harmed, 'tis only what they deserved . . . and you too, for that matter. What the devil do you think you were doing in the midst of that rabble? You might have been killed!"

The curt words brought Pip's head snapping up. Certainly she was grateful he had appeared when he had, and she was well aware he had doubtlessly saved her life with his quick, decisive action. But that didn't mean she would allow him to scold her as if she was an errant child. She was about to let him know precisely what she thought of such high-handed behavior when she heard a second voice complain, "Well, I hope you are satisfied, St. Ives! I was cut by a piece of glass, and now I've got blood on m'cravat. 'Tis ruined!"

She glanced over at the man sitting next to St. Ives, her eyes widening in dismay as she recognized Tobias Flanders's petulant expression. Her jaw dropped as the very real potential for scandal suddenly struck her. She was as good as ruined.

"You'll live." Alex's voice was singularly lacking in sympathy as he continued studying Miss Lambert's expression. Mortification was replacing the anger that had been in the light green depths of her eyes only moments before, and he felt a grim satisfaction at the thought that she was not wholly lost to the sensibilities.

"I was lucky not to have been killed," Toby continued, warming to his grievances. "The rock that fellow chucked at me was as big as m'fist, and—"

"We will let you out at the next corner, Flanders, so that you may seek immediate medical attention," Alex interrupted, his tone derisive. "I wouldn't want your death on my conscience."

"Eh?" Toby looked puzzled. "No such thing, St. Ives. Not about to stick m'spoon in the wall and all that. But dash it, m'cravat is ruined and—"

"And naturally you wish to slink home and repair the damage before you are seen; I understand perfectly." Alex rapped the top of the carriage with the cane he had been carrying. "Stop here," he instructed the driver.

"But—"

"No more, Tobias." Alex used Toby's given name with cold emphasis. "I think we are agreed the less said at this point, the better. To anyone. I trust you take my meaning?"

Toby's eyes strayed to Miss Lambert's strained features. "Oh. Well, as to that, your lordship, hope to say I ain't a tattler. That is, I know when to hold m'tongue and all that."

"I sincerely hope so." Alex was already pushing open the door as the carriage rolled to a halt. "I like and respect Colford, and I should dislike killing his nephew and heir merely because he couldn't keep his mouth closed."

The implicit threat in the coldly spoken words had Toby paling in fear. "Yes, m'lord! That is . . . no, your lordship! I shall be silent as the grave, sir, you may depend 'pon it!"

"Oh, I do, Flanders, I do." Alex smiled as the other man tumbled hurriedly out the door. "And so does your life. Remember that."

Moments later the carriage resumed its journey, and an uneasy silence filled the interior. Finally Alex broke the silence, his voice coolly controlled as he said, "I think we may rely upon Flanders's fear of me to keep his tongue from wagging maliciously. Which means we need only fear its wagging from sheer stupidity—a far more likely possibility, I fear."

An unwilling smile touched the corners of Pip's mouth. "I had noticed he has a regrettable tendency toward loquacity, your lordship," she said, studying him from beneath her lashes.

"He is an idiot," Alex retorted bluntly, "but he will remain silent if he values his hide."

His implacable tone shocked Pip. "You would really call him out?" she asked weakly, understanding at last that he was in dead earnest. "But I thought he was your friend."

Alex settled against his seat with a negligent shrug. "Colford is far more my friend than he is. But in answer to your question, yes, I would really call him out. I am a man of my word, Miss Lambert, and I never say anything without meaning it."

There was a threat in his silky words Pip deemed wisest to ignore. Drawing the remnants of her pride about her, she managed a cool smile. "It seems then, sir, that I am doubly in your debt. You have not only saved my neck, but my reputation as well."

"Then you are aware of the risks you ran with this

juvenile prank. Good. I was beginning to think you a complete idiot."

Pip's smile vanished so abruptly it might have been wiped from her face. "Idiot?" she repeated in furious tones. "How dare you! I am an intellectual!"

"You are as half-witted as a moonling if you thought you could scrape through this afternoon's adventure without suffering any consequences," he snapped, his anger flaring. He'd seen what was happening as he dragged her to safety, and the sight of it had sickened him. Men and women being trampled underfoot by the frenzied mob, to say nothing of the bloodletting being enjoyed by the rougher elements of the crowd.

When he considered what might have happened to her had he not been there to rescue her, he felt like shaking her until her hair came tumbling down from its prim chignon. It was already halfway there, he thought, noting the tendrils of chestnut hair that were curling about her flushed face.

"The only consequence I seem to be suffering at this moment is a great deal of impertinence on your part, your lordship," Pip returned, every bit as regal in her fury as Belle might have been. "I scarce know you, sir, and I deeply resent your presuming to tell me how to conduct my life!"

"*Touché,* Miss Lambert."

"What?"

A hard smile touched Alex's eyes at the look of angry confusion on her face. "Or perhaps I should say tit for tat," he added, crossing his feet and regarding her with cool challenge. "I agree that we are virtual strangers, yet that didn't stop you from criticizing me, did it?"

Embarrassed color washed over Pip's cheeks, and she suddenly found herself unable to meet his steady blue eyes. "I was but twitting you, sir," she muttered, her eyes stealing toward the window. It was indeed shattered, and she wondered how she should broach the matter of replacing it. Instinct warned her he would doubtlessly rail at the very suggestion.

"Perhaps. But I do not choose to view aspersions cast upon my honor as a joking matter."

She winced at the cold irony in his voice. "I wasn't casting aspersions on your honor," she denied, still unable to look at him. "That is the problem with you Tories. You're all so pompous and stuffy without a whit of humor among you, and—" Her voice broke off as his lean fingers curled around her chin, turning her head gently but inexorably toward him.

"Do not drag politics into this, hoyden," he said, his eyes meeting hers. "This is between you and me. I would know why you judged and condemned me in a single look."

His compelling words forced Pip to blurt out the truth—or at least as much of the truth as she dared speak. "Because you have what I have always wanted, and you squander it without thought."

Her answer surprised Alex. "And what do I have that you so desire? My title? If so, I must tell you it is only mine through default. Had my brother lived—"

"I wasn't referring to your blasted title!" she snapped, jerking her chin free from his gentle grasp. "As if I should ever care for such paltry concerns!"

"Then what are you referring to?" he pressed, determined to learn the mystery of her antipathy.

For a moment Pip greatly feared she would disgrace herself by dissolving into tears. This was her most private desire, the part of herself she held secret from all but a few. Never in a thousand years could she ever imagine sharing these thoughts with any man—especially a man like St. Ives. Yet what choice did she have? She took a deep breath, her hands clenching in her lap as she said, "Imagine yourself on the outside looking in, denied the one thing you want above all else. And then imagine being told that rather than resenting this deprivation, you ought to be grateful, that this is the natural order of things, and you can never hope to change it."

"I still do not know what you are talking about," Alex said, hearing the pain in her voice but still not understanding it. "What has been denied you?"

"The franchise," she blurted out, her eyes bright as she met his startled gaze. "You can vote, which is something I can never hope to obtain, even in my wildest dreams. What is more, you are a member of Parliament. You pass laws which influence every aspect of our lives, and yet you can't even be bothered to attend the debating sessions. How can I not resent you?"

There was a moment of shocked silence before Alex was able to find his voice. "You wish the vote?" he asked at last. "Flanders said as much, but I thought he was exaggerating for effect, as he often does."

A bitter smile pulled at Pip's mouth. "I think we have already agreed that society gossip is more reliable than one may first suppose," she said, referring to their conversation at Almack's. "I did indeed once voice that foolish desire, and was thoroughly condemned for my audacity. Since then I have come to accept that we women are viewed as naught but ornaments, denied even the smallest voice in the world in which we are forced to live."

Alex didn't know quite how to respond to this, and so he said nothing. Miss Lambert was possessed of the unerring ability to overset him at every turn, and he was not certain he cared for that—or her, for that matter. But he did respect her, and accepting that, he knew he could not continue with the wager. He opened his lips to confess all when he saw blood seeping through the shoulder of her pelisse.

"My God, you've been hurt!"

Pip glanced down at her shoulder. "Oh, that." She

It particularly galled him to forfeit his wager to such a creature, but clenching his jaw, he prepared to do just that.

"I am glad you are here, Kingsford, for it will spare me the trouble of seeking you out. Do you prefer to take your winnings in cash, or will you accept a draft from my bank?"

That drove the look of sneering insolence from Kingsford's face. "What the devil are you talking about?" he demanded.

"You know full well what I am talking about," Alex snapped, determined not to mention Miss Lambert's name. "I have lost, and I wish to settle up my account. I believe the wager was for five hundred pounds?"

"What?" Kingsford scrambled to his feet. "Never say the wench turned you down!"

"Most definitely, and in a manner there was no mistaking," Alex answered, assuring himself it wasn't really a lie. He had the feeling that were he to issue such an invitation, Miss Lambert would hand him back his head in a twinkling.

"Well, I'm floored," Kingsford said, proving his point by collapsing on to the chair and gazing at Alex with watery blue eyes. "I was positive you would win!"

"As was I," Alex agreed. "Which only proves the old saw about pride going before a fall. Now as to payment—"

"But I was so certain." Kingsford thrust a hand through his blond hair arranged *a la* Byron. "I mean, a viscount and all. How could she say no? The gel is daft, that's what. A Bedlamite. I am ruined."

His despairing tones made Alex stiffen in a cold rush of awareness. "What do you mean *you* are ruined?" he asked, keeping his voice steady only with a great deal of effort. " 'Tis I who has lost to you."

"Here, perhaps, but I am referring to the bet at White's. I wagered three thousand pounds on your winning the bet."

"You did *what?*" Alex was on his feet and across the rug, grabbing Kingsford by the lapels and hauling him out of the chair. "Damn you, Kingsford, I shall call you out for this!"

"Well, what else was I to do?" Reginald asked plaintively, his eyes wide. "The odds was four to one against you. I stood to make a cool twelve thousand pounds, but as 'tis now, I shall be obliged to sell off my cattle to cover my marker."

Alex's fingers tightened around the rich velvet of Kingsford's jacket. "Blast it, Kingsford, you gave me your word that—" He broke off suddenly. "The odds were against me?" he asked in stunned disbelief.

"Four to one," Reginald repeated obligingly. "They was slightly lower at Brooks where you are better known, but—"

"How the devil did word of this get out?" Alex demanded, his head reeling with a mixture of fury and mortification. He wasn't sure what made him the angrier: that Kingsford had broken his word, or that the betting had gone against him. It was the most humiliating moment of his life.

"Can't say as I know, your lordship." Kingsford took advantage of Alex's stunned senses to gain his freedom. He pried Alex's fingers from his jacket and took a cautious step backwards. "All I know is that the wager's common knowledge in all the clubs."

Alex swore furiously beneath his breath, realizing there was no way he could hope to quietly end the wager. "And Miss Lambert's name is being mentioned?" he asked, his fingers clenching and unclenching with the need to make someone pay for this contretemps.

"Certainly not." Kingsford drew himself up haughtily. "We are gentlemen, after all. She is being set down only as Mme. X. Of course, once she appears with you at Carlton House the cat will be well and truly out of the bag, but that can't be helped, I suppose."

"She won't be appearing with me at Carlton House,"

Alex said, rubbing a hand across a head that was now throbbing. "I told you, she refused my invitation."

"Ah, but a woman's no is never really final, is it?" Kingsford said, sidling closer. "The dear ladies are forever changing their minds about everything, and one mustn't ever accept their decisions as definite."

"Miss Lambert is not like most women," Alex answered, thinking they were the truest words he had spoken since entering the club.

"Indeed, which is precisely what makes the bet so interesting. If she were an ordinary deb, what would be the point? But as the worst bluestocking in London, she is a prize well worth the winning. Do you not agree?"

He thought about the passion in her eyes as she had spoken of her longing to vote, the proud way she had lifted her chin as she defied him. "More than worth the winning," he agreed roughly. "But that doesn't change the fact that she refused me. I am sorry about the three thousand pounds, but—"

"The prince's ball is still some weeks ahead," Kingsford said, cutting eagerly into Alex's speech. "There is ample opportunity for you to change her mind if you but try." He leaned closer, speaking to Alex in a man-to-man voice. "You really don't wish it said that you allowed a *woman* to best you—do you?"

Alex flinched, his face reddening. "Of course not, but—"

"Well, there you are," Kingsford concluded with a happy nod. "There is nothing left to be said. The bet stands as it is."

Pip was disappointed the next day to learn poor Belle was still indisposed, but upon reflection she decided it might be for the best. Even though they shared many of the same unconventional beliefs, there were times when her friend could be depressingly proper. She would doubtlessly read her a severe scold were she ever to learn how close she'd come to disaster. A student of

Shakespeare, Pip agreed with his observation that discretion was the better part of valor.

The incident at Mayfield Gardens, which *The Times* insisted upon calling a riot, occupied several columns of the morning paper, and Pip was perusing a rather inaccurate description of events when her aunt paid a surprising visit to the breakfast table.

"Good morning, ma'am," Pip said, taking pains to hide the paper from the older lady. "You are abroad early this day. I trust all is well?"

"Oh yes, quite well, my dear." Mrs. Beachton gave her one of her vague smiles as she shook out her linen napkin. "I have an early appointment at my modiste's, that is all."

"Early indeed, if it has you poking your nose below-stairs at the unfashionable hour of ten o'clock," Pip responded with a silent sigh of relief. She'd greatly feared her aunt had somehow learned the truth of yesterday afternoon and was about to give her yet another lecture on decorum.

"It *is* an unfashionable hour," Mrs. Beachton agreed, hiding a yawn behind her fist, "but Madame is so busy these days that one must book appointments weeks in advance for a fitting. You were quite right to recommend her to me, by the by, and I am most appreciative. You always seem to be *au courant* on such matters. That is why I do not understand . . ."

"Do not understand what, Aunt?" Pip asked when Mrs. Beachton's voice trailed to a halt.

Her aunt's lined face suffused with color, and she lowered her eyes to the cup of tea the footman had prepared for her. "You must not think me critical, my dear," she muttered, nervously fingering the gilded rim of her cup. "You are a grown lady, after all, and 'tis your own affair what you choose to wear. But I still do not understand why you insist upon dressing like a governess. 'Tis not as if you don't have any clothing sense, for you dressed most charmingly while your papa was still alive, and—"

"I wore the gowns my father selected and paid for, Aunt," Pip interrupted, her green eyes growing cold as she recalled the way her father had dictated every aspect of her wardrobe. "Now that he is dead, I dress to please myself."

Mrs. Beachton's color deepened at the lack of filial tenderness in Pip's chilly tones. "Be that as it may, Phillipa, I fail to see why you dress in so uncomplimentary a fashion. I know you consider yourself a bluestocking, but that does not mean you must needs dress so poorly. Only look at your friend Belle; she is every bit as intellectual as you, yet she is always dressed in the first stare of fashion."

"I am not Belle, Aunt," Pip replied, striving to keep the hurt out of her voice. She and her aunt had had this conversation many times in the past, and she was aware that the other woman found her behavior mystifying. Pip did not know how to tell her that there were times when she was equally as mystified. She only knew that every time she thought about exchanging one of her prim brown or gray gowns for something more attractive, she would hear her father's sneering voice telling her that even though she was as plain as a pikestaff, he expected her to dress as fashionably as possible so that she might attract an offer of marriage. It was all a female was good for, he would inevitably add with a bitter laugh, and considering the blunt he had spent on her, it was the least she could do.

"I know that, dearest, but still 'twould not hurt so much to have one fashionable gown, would it?" Mrs. Beachton pressed, peering anxiously at Pip's strained features. "Something in a pretty rose, perhaps, or an emerald green to bring out your eyes. You have quite the loveliest eyes, and it seems a great pity to me that you don't show them to better advantage."

Pip shook off her black memories. "I could always

take to wearing kohl like an actress, ma'am," she suggested with a bright smile. "That would show them to their best advantage, would it not?"

Her aunt gave her a severe look. "I suppose you think you are being clever," she said in a reproachful voice. "But I assure you, you are not. Now, about your new wardrobe . . ."

"You said one gown, Aunt," Pip said, neither agreeing nor disagreeing with the older woman.

"Yes, but one cannot wear *just* a gown, can one?" Mrs. Beachton pointed out with a practical nod. "There are gloves and slippers to be considered, to say nothing of a pelisse, a bonnet, a reticule, and of course, jewelry. Your father left you the most beautiful emeralds and a stunning set of pearls and diamonds, but I can't say as I've ever seen you wear them. Haven't pawned them, have you?" She bent a suspicious frown on Pip.

"No, Aunt, I have not," Pip replied, her eyes twinkling. "How much do you think they would fetch?"

"Phillipa!"

"I am sorry," Pip apologized, chuckling at her aunt's horrified expression. "But 'twill be something to remember should I ever find myself in the suds."

"Hmph." Mrs. Beachton gave a loud sniff. "Well? Will you be accompanying me to Madame Duvall's, or must I go alone?"

Pip was about to give her usual refusal when she fell silent. Perhaps one ensemble wouldn't be so terrible, she decided reluctantly, and after yesterday she did need a new pelisse. The maid had declared the old one quite ruined, and she'd had the torn, bloodstained brown velvet smuggled from the house.

"Very well, ma'am," she said at last. "I shall be happy to accompany you. But"—she held up a warning finger before her aunt could burst into excited speech—"I shall purchase but the one pelisse, and nothing else."

"Certainly, dearest." Mrs. Beachton was so delighted

at Pip's unexpected capitulation that she was willing to agree to anything. "It shall be just as you like."

"If 'twas just as I liked, I shouldn't be going at all," Pip grumbled, her interest growing as she finished her meal in thoughtful silence. Perhaps she might order something in the new military style, with a wide, notched collar and just a touch of gold frogging on the front. The image was unexpectedly pleasing, but not so pleasing was the traitorous part of her mind that persisted in wondering what Lord St. Ives would think of her in her new finery.

A strange carriage was pulled up in front of the house as Pip and her aunt returned from their shopping expedition. "I wonder who that might be," Pip said, as she stepped down from their hired hack. "Were you expecting anyone?"

"Indeed not," Mrs. Beachton replied, handing her purchases to the footman who had hurried out to assist them. "Today is Saturday, and none of my friends would . . . heavens! 'Tis St. Ives! I recognize his crest!"

Pip stepped closer to the glistening black carriage, studying the scarlet and gold coat of arms painted on the door. It depicted a unicorn and a dragon locked in what looked to be a fond embrace, although she gathered it was supposed to be something a trifle more lethal. She'd always considered crests and monograms to be the ultimate in conceit, and she was vaguely disappointed that the viscount should choose to flaunt his position. Evidently he wasn't so sanguine about the title as he let on, she decided with a flash of cynicism.

"Why are you just standing there, goose?" Her aunt interrupted her revery with a sharp poke in the ribs. "It is obvious his lordship has called upon us, and it wouldn't do to keep him waiting while you gawk at his carriage!"

"I wasn't gawking," Pip denied, her expression carefully composed as she turned toward the house. "And as his lordship has already been waiting for an undetermined length of time, I do not see that a few minutes more should matter."

Such a callous attitude toward one's visitors set the older woman back a pace, and she launched into a hasty lecture on the proprieties as she and Pip hurried up the wide, stone steps of the brick town house.

Pip scarce heard her aunt's scolding voice, her mind awhirl at the thought of Lord St. Ives waiting for her. She wondered why he had come, and her jaw set in a determined line as she considered the most logical explanation. If the wretch had come to ring a peal over her head, she would dump a pot of tea over his. The devil with her aunt's dictum that, should they deign to call upon one, lords of whatever rank were to be treated with smiling deference.

In the blue and white drawing room, Alex heard their arrival with impatient relief. He'd only been waiting a quarter-hour, but he was already straining at the bit to be gone. He'd deliberately timed his arrival at a time when most ladies of society were sure to be at home, only to find that Miss Lambert had gone shopping with her aunt. Shopping! He shook his head at the thought. Somehow he'd never imagined his belligerent bluestocking engaging in such a typically feminine pursuit.

The sudden vision of her solemnly examining bolts of cloth and lace brought an angry scowl to his face. He'd spent the better part of the night laying his strategy, before reaching the conclusion that the only way to achieve his objective was to cease regarding her as a person. It was like being in a battle, he'd decided. A soldier who thought of his enemy as a fellow human being could never do some of the brutal, terrible things that victory and survival sometimes dictated. Miss Lambert may not be his enemy per se, but the same conditions applied. He wouldn't forget that again.

The sound of the door opening brought him swinging around, a cool smile of welcome already on his lips.

"Ah, Mrs. Beachton, Miss Lambert." He greeted each one with a low bow. "I trust you will forgive me for making free of your parlor while I was waiting?"

"Certainly, your lordship, if you will forgive us for not being here to receive you." Mrs. Beachton bustled forward to drop a curtsey before Pip could speak. "Naturally, had I known of your visit I would have put off our trip." Here a pointed look was directed at Pip.

"No need to cast daggers at me, Aunt Morwenna." Pip's smile was every bit as cool as his as she dropped a polite curtsey. "How nice to see you again, sir. I must say you do have the habit of appearing in the most surprising of places."

Alex knew this to be a taunting reference to yesterday, and ignored it with another flashing smile. "Surprise is the spice of life, Miss Lambert; did you not know that? But actually, I have a very good reason for calling upon you in so ill-bred a manner. I was anxious about Miss Portham. Is she still ill?"

"Belle is ill?" Mrs. Beachton turned alarmed eyes on Pip. "Oh dear, Phillipa, why did you not tell me?"

"It is but a migraine, ma'am," she soothed, lest her aunt take it into her head to rush over to Belle's house on Half Moon Street, "although I fear 'tis plaguing her most dreadfully." She gave St. Ives a cool look. "I shall tell her you asked after her, your lordship. I am sure she will be most gratified."

"Will she?" Alex was amused by her regal air.

"Indeed," Pip replied, thinking Belle would doubtlessly be a great deal more than gratified by the viscount's interest. Perhaps this plot of hers had some hope of succeeding after all, she told herself, and then wondered why the realization didn't please her.

The maid soon appeared with the tea, and they spent the next hour in quiet conversation. The charm that had helped St. Ives establish his rakish reputation was much in evidence, and even Pip found herself warming to his slow smile and the wry way he mocked himself. She'd found most men to be too puffed up with their own consequence to admit to any weakness, and she liked the fact that St. Ives could do so with such good humor.

"You fell off your horse in front of Wellington?" She laughed as he concluded a particularly humorous anecdote. "Whatever did he say?"

"That it was a good thing I was in the infantry rather than the cavalry," Alex said, smiling at the memory. "Unfortunately, my commander was less amused, and I was restricted to my quarters for the next fortnight."

"How cruel of him," Pip sympathized, although her eyes twinkled to think of the viscount sent to his rooms like an errant schoolboy.

"But necessary. In an army good discipline is all."

"Quite so, my lord." Mrs. Beachton bobbed her head in agreement. "Many was the time I can recall hearing my late husband commenting on that very subject. Why, I remember once . . ." And she lapsed into a rambling monologue concerning the general's view on everything from the correct way to discipline troops to the shocking conduct of the royals.

Alex, who had less fond memories of his blustering and inept commanding officer, listened with every evidence of interest, even as he was planning his next move. When Mrs. Beachton paused to take a breath, he moved quickly, turning to Miss Lambert with a polite smile. "We were speaking of Miss Portham earlier, ma'am, and I was wondering if you and she were planning to attend the lecture at Lady Witherspoon's?"

"The lecture on civic improvement?" His question caught Pip by surprise. "Certainly, milord. Lady Witherspoon is a particular friend of ours, and the subject is one that much interests Belle."

"As it does me. I thought, with your aunt's permission, of course"—he flashed Mrs. Beachton a winning smile—"that I would lend you my escort."

Pip's jaw dropped in utter amazement. After yesterday's debacle she would have thought he would have been more than happy to see the back of her. Yet here he was, as proper as a parson at tea, offering to accompany Belle and her to a lecture on civic improvement. What on earth was going on? she wondered, her eyes narrowing in sudden suspicion.

"That is very gracious of you, sir," she began, knowing Belle would throttle her if she were to refuse. "I am sure Belle—"

". . . would be delighted to accept," Mrs. Beachton finished quickly, fearing her foolish niece was about to reject the viscount's very generous offer. "As is Phillipa, I am sure. And I must tell you 'twould make my own mind a great deal easier. I quite worry about my girls attending those unseemly lectures. Only look at what happened yesterday! Thank heavens they had the good sense not to attend after all."

So the minx *had* lied to her aunt, Alex thought, shooting Pip an arch look. "Yes," he drawled mockingly, "thank heavens for that."

The rest of the hour passed in relative peace, and soon it was time to leave. Since he had achieved his primary objective—securing Miss Lambert's permission to escort her and her icy friend to their silly lecture—he decided to stage a strategic withdrawal. It was a trick he had learned on the peninsula: hit and run. It helped defeat the French, he reminded himself with a grim smile, and there was no reason to think it would prove any less effective against a stubborn and argumentive bluestocking.

Finally the elegant gold clock on the mantelpiece tolled the hour, and Alex rose to his feet. "I am afraid that I must be leaving," he said, treating each lady to his warmest smile. "Miss Lambert, if you would be so good as to escort me to the door, we can settle upon our plans for Tuesday."

"Certainly, sir," Pip answered, murmuring a quick apology to her aunt before guiding him out into the hallway. She stood quietly as he retrieved his hat and gloves from the butler, waiting until they were alone before turning to him with a rueful smile.

"Neatly done, your lordship, although there was no need for you to include my aunt in your machinations. I had already decided to accept your kind offer."

"Had you?" Alex studied her upturned face, silently congratulating himself on his strategy of winning her friendship by playing on her interest in politics. On another woman he might have used flattery or even jewels, but he knew such lures wouldn't succeed with her. There was only one thing which seemed to raise Miss Lambert's passions, and he would use that interest to throw them together at every opportunity.

"Yes, your lordship, I had," Pip answered, wondering what had brought that hard look to his face. "I'd also like to thank you for not telling my aunt the truth about yesterday. "I fear she tends to worry about me."

"Not without cause, 'twould seem," he replied, pushing his black thoughts to one side. "One can only hope the lecture at Lady Witherspoon's will prove somewhat less . . . exuberant."

Pip's eyes filled with laughter. "It will be dull as dishwater, I assure you," she promised him solemnly. "Are you quite sure you wish to attend?"

"Quite sure," he answered, thinking she was rather pretty when she smiled like that. "If only so that I might keep an eye on you. You do seem to possess a remarkable propensity for attracting disaster. That reminds me. How is your shoulder?"

"Fine," she replied, trying not to take umbrage at his wry observation. "As I said, it was only a scratch."

"If you say so." He sounded doubtful, his eyes straying to the object under discussion. She was wearing a prim gown of gray cambric, but beneath the thin material he thought he could detect a thick bandage. Unable to stop himself, he laid his fingertip against it.

"I'm sorry."

Pip's eyes widened at his gruff tone. "About what?"

"This." He stroked her shoulder lightly, his dark blue eyes flashing as they met hers. "I should have taken better care of you."

She flushed in sudden confusion, not knowing what to think. She was so accustomed to looking after herself it had never occurred to her to look to another for protection, and certainly never to a man. For a moment she felt the traitorous desire to accept the silent strength he was offering her, but in the next moment her common sense reasserted itself and she took a determined step backwards.

"Nonsense, Lord St. Ives," she said in a firm voice. "It is my own fault I was hurt, not yours. I am no schoolroom miss who requires looking after, and I assure you that I am more than capable of taking care of myself."

"Are you?" Her defiant words had brought a cold smile to his lips.

"Yes." She raised her chin, her eyes meeting his as if daring him to disagree.

"Then I shall see you and Miss Portham on Tuesday," he answered calmly, giving her a mocking bow. "My best to your charming aunt," and he strode out the door with an arrogant swagger that made Pip long to screech with rage.

The visit to Lady Witherspoon's was but the first in a series of outings as the viscount spent the next week escorting Pip and Belle to a variety of lectures and meetings. At first Pip suspected him of amusing himself at their expense, but when he showed no sign of flagging, she was forced to reconsider the matter.

Perhaps there was more to St. Ives than a handsome face and a rather arrogant disposition, she decided one afternoon, her dark brows gathered in a frown as she stared out the window of her study. She'd already reached the conclusion they'd misjudged his character, and it was entirely possible his sudden interest in politics was genuine. Certainly Belle seemed to think so, she thought with a sigh, recalling her friend's mounting enthusiasm for the viscount's company. In fact, had it been any woman other than Belle, she would have accused her of having developed a *tendresse* for St. Ives.

The realization brought her up short, and for one wild moment she wondered if Belle had indeed fallen victim to the viscount's winning charm. There had been a certain softness about her of late, and only yesterday Pip had caught her friend staring out the window, the oddest look in her golden eyes. What if . . . ?

A sudden commotion at the door shattered Pip's speculations, and she turned around just as Belle stormed into the room. One look at her friend's flushed face and flashing eyes and Pip leaped to her feet in alarm. "What is it?" she demanded, fearing some dreadful calamity must have occurred. "What has happened?"

"That wretch!" Belle responded, all trace of The Golden Icicle melted by the heat of her anger. "That miserable, lying, deceitful wretch! You were right about him from the very start; he is a rake! A . . . a . . . dissipated dandy!"

"Who on earth are you talking about?" Pip demanded, bewildered by Belle's uncharacteristic display of temper. She knew of only one man who could move Belle to such passion, and the last she had heard, Colford was in the country tending one of his far-flung estates.

"St. Ives, of course!" Belle snapped, the skirts of her bright blue gown swirling about her as she paced up and down the length of the study. "Oh! And to think I was actually beginning to believe there might be some hope for him after all! The scheming knave! How he must be laughing at the pair of us!"

A frisson of alarm shot through Pip. "What about St. Ives?" she asked cautiously, all of her earlier doubts returning to haunt her. "What has he done?"

"Done? I'll tell you what he has done! He has wagered five hundred pounds that he will win your agreement to accompany him to the regent's ball! *That's* what he has done!"

Five

Ribbon decoration

"**H**e bet *what?*" Pip stared at Belle in shock.

"That you would accompany him to Carlton House," Belle answered, only too happy to tell Pip of the viscount's perfidity, the details of which she had just learned. "Can you imagine anything so lowering? As if a female of your superior intellect and breeding would ever deign to poke her nose into that den of iniquitous Tories!"

"But whyever should he want to do such a thing?" Pip demanded, disbelief giving way to fury.

Despite her anger, Belle was first and foremost a person who played fair. "Well, to give the devil his due, the wager was not wholly his idea," she admitted gruffly. "It was more or less forced upon him by that idiot Toby Flanders and that awful fop Reginald Kingsford—not that that in any way excuses him, mind. Those two are too mutton-brained to be held responsible, but St. Ives is another story altogether."

"So he is," Pip agreed, struggling to control her rapidly rising temper. First she would learn all the facts, she promised herself furiously, and then she would storm over to St. Ives's home and box his ears until he howled. She drew a deep breath and gave Belle a cool look.

"May I ask how you came to learn of this?" she said, taking pride in her icy control.

"One of my friends told me," Belle said, settling on one of the comfortable side chairs set before the fireplace. "Her employer's husband was speaking of it, and she thought I should know. Nor is the wager the half of it."

"There's *more?*" Pip was horrified.

"Unfortunately," Belle said with a sigh and went on to lay the whole of it at Pip's feet. When she finished at last, she sat back in the chair, her expression remorseful as she studied her friend. "I am sorry, my dear. If I hadn't dragooned you into introducing me to the viscount, this might never have happened. 'Tis all my fault, and I cannot tell you how—"

"The betting was four to one against St. Ives?" Pip interrupted, her lips quivering as she fought the laughter that had been welling up in her since Belle had finished her story. In the end, however, her odd sense of humor won out, and she collapsed against the plump cushions of the settee, holding her sides as the laughter rolled out of her.

Of all the reactions Belle had expected, amusement wasn't one of them. She stared at Pip in startled dismay. "Phillipa!" she exclaimed, shocked. "Didn't you hear what I just said? St. Ives has all but ruined you! 'Tis hardly a matter for levity!"

"Yes, Belle, it most certainly is," Pip managed when she could draw a steady breath. "It is in fact quite the funniest thing I have ever heard in my life!"

"Funny?" Golden sparks flew from Belle's eyes. "When the man has made you the laughingstock of London?"

"Oh, don't be so stuffy, Belle!" Pip said, wiping her streaming eyes with the heel of her hand. "Only *think* for a moment. Is it me society is laughing at, or is it St. Ives?"

Belle was about to contest the charge of stuffiness when Pip's words stopped her. "What do you mean?" she asked.

"Well," Pip began carefully, "if it was me, then I would indeed be the object of much speculation and malicious tattle—the silly little bluestocking foolish enough to believe that a man of St. Ives's reputation would actually want to escort her to the premier event of the Season. But that's not how the betting is going, is it?"

"No, but—"

"In fact, if the books at White's are any indication, I am the favored filly in this race. Don't you see?" she exclaimed when Belle continued staring at her in confusion. "*I* am not the one the *ton* is snickering at—*he* is!"

Belle's eyes grew wide. Her mouth opened, closed, and in another moment she was laughing every bit as hard as Pip. "I hadn't thought of it like that," she admitted, her cheeks flushed with amusement. "But you are quite right. St. Ives must have been furious when he learned of it!"

"Raving mad, I should think," Pip agreed, grinning to think of the viscount's fury when he heard of the odds. "And it certainly explains his sudden interest in politics. I was rather suspicious about that."

Belle's smile vanished. "The beast!" she fumed, rising to her feet and resuming her restless pacing. "*I* was completely taken in by his posing. I genuinely believed him to be capable of concern for others—more the fool me."

"Don't be so hard on yourself," Pip advised, troubled by the bitterness in Belle's normally cool voice. She remembered what she had been thinking just before Belle had burst into her study, and her own amusement faded. She rose to her feet and hurried to her friend's side.

"Belle," she said, laying a consoling hand on her arm and studying her face anxiously, "you don't *love* St. Ives, do you?"

"What?" Belle was staring at her as if she were speaking Greek.

"I mean," Pip clarified, "it would hardly be surprising if you did. His lordship is most handsome, and when he puts his mind to it I am sure he could charm the birds from the trees, but—"

"Don't be absurd!" Belle interrupted, her dark blond eyebrows descending in an impatient scowl. "Of course I don't love him! I don't love any man. He is naught to me but the means to an end."

The tight coil of fear in Pip's stomach unravelled with relief. It was one thing for her to be harmed by the wager, for she was genuinely unconcerned with what society might think. Belle, however, was another matter, and Pip would not stand for her friend's being hurt in any way. If Belle had fallen in love with the viscount because of his silly pose, Pip would have made his life a living hell.

"Well, that is good to hear," she said, stepping back with a smile. "For a moment I was beginning to fear you had taken leave of your senses and were truly in love with the wretch."

"Never," Belle assured her, regaining her customary coolness. "I have already explained at some length that the only marriage I would ever consider is one of convenience. Not that it matters with St. Ives. I shouldn't have him now if he promised to make me prime minister of England!"

"Why?"

"Why?" Belle repeated, blinking at Pip. "Why do you think? Because of the bet, you silly creature! We can scarce associate with him now that we know the truth!"

"At the risk of sounding like a simpleton, I must once again ask you why," Pip said, folding her arms across her chest and regarding Belle with aplomb. "He is still by far the best candidate we have, and it seems unfair to disqualify him for something which even you admit is not really his fault."

"Perhaps not," Belle said, confused by Pip's unexpected championing of the viscount. "But I still do not like that he would seek to use our interest in politics in order to get close to you. It bespeaks a treacherous and untrustworthy mind that—"

"Whereas you, on the other hand, have been completely and utterly truthful with the viscount from the very first."

Pip's sardonic words made Belle frown. "What are you saying?"

"That you can hardly rail against St. Ives for being dishonest when you yourself have been less than forthcoming with him," Pip said, her smile gentle despite her admonishing words. "Rather a case of the kettle calling the pot black, would you not agree?"

If the sour expression on Belle's face was any indication, it was a point she would have very much liked to argue, but in the end the honesty and integrity that Pip had always admired won out, and she gave Pip a sheepish smile. "Put that way, I suppose my objections *are* rather ridiculous," she agreed. "But what about you? How can you bear to tolerate his company, knowing he is only using you? Aren't you angry?"

"Furious," Pip admitted, with a wide smile that hid the last trace of pain she had felt when she first learned of the wager and St. Ives's part in it. "But I console myself with the knowledge that we are also using him. Besides, all's fair in war, and if we are clever enough to keep our heads, then this wager can only work to our advantage. After all, in order to win my agreement to accompany him to the ball, he will have to spend a great deal of time in our company, will he not?"

Belle considered this for a long moment before her eyes took on a mischievous sparkle. "You," she accused with a soft laugh, "are a wicked and devious woman."

"Quite so." Pip executed a low curtsey. "Just the sort to deal with a wicked and devious lord. Unless you have developed a horror of him?" she asked, her eyes flashing to Belle's face as the thought suddenly occurred to her.

Belle considered that and shook her head. "No. In fact, I feel he may be redeemable. He gave me a hundred pounds for my school, did I tell you?"

"No, you did not," Pip said, feeling faintly surprised. Not by the viscount's generosity, but by the fact Belle had told him of her secret charity. She had known Belle for over two years before her friend had finally told her of the school she was starting for the orphaned children of England's soldiers. That she had already told the viscount was vaguely hurtful, although for the life of her Pip could not say why.

Belle was studying Pip with a troubled frown. "Are you quite certain you're not hurt?" she asked gently. "After all, you are much better acquainted with the viscount than me."

For a moment Pip considered lying, if only to spare Belle's feelings, but in the end she decided her friend deserved the truth. "A little," she admitted, turning away from that too-knowing gaze. "As I have already said, his lordship is most handsome, and I suppose I allowed myself to be ... taken in by his charms.

"But you were never enamored of him?"

That brought Pip spinning around in shock. "Certainly not!" she denied, horrified Belle should ask such a thing. "You know how I feel about men!"

Belle was careful to hide a grin at the vehemence in Pip's voice. "I thought I did," she said dryly, "but I was beginning to have my doubts. I can see now I was mistaken."

"I should say so," Pip grumbled, only slightly mollified. "Might I remind you the objective of this farce is to get *you* leg-shackled to St. Ives? *I* have no intention of taking a husband. Ever."

"So you have said."

"And if I were mad enough to contemplate such a

thing," Pip continued, ignoring the laughter in Belle's eyes, "I certainly wouldn't choose an arrogant rake like St. Ives! The man is too domineering by half."

"Yes, he is that," Belle agreed, tilting her head to one side. "But I have decided that a touch of arrogance in a gentleman may not be such a bad thing after all."

Pip perked up at that. "Really?" she drawled, sending Belle what could only be termed a smirk. "I shall be certain to tell Lord Colford that the very next time I see him."

Belle stiffened in instant umbrage. "I said a *touch* of arrogance, Phillipa," she informed Pip frostily. "His lordship hardly qualifies on that account. He is as arrogant as a prince and as impudent as a king. I will thank you not to mention him again."

"Very well, Belle," Pip agreed. She enjoyed twitting Belle on the matter of the earl, but at the moment they had more serious matters to consider. "So, you think we ought to continue as we have?" she asked, forcing herself to sound as coolly controlled as Belle herself.

"It seems the most logical thing to do," Belle said after a thoughtful pause. "As you say, he is the most likely candidate."

"But what of the wager?" Pip demanded, determined that there be no question in Belle's mind.

Belle shrugged. "I agree with you; it can only aid our cause so long as we keep our heads. And, of course, so long as you refuse the viscount's invitation to join him at Carlton House." Here she sent Pip a teasing smile.

"I shall be as immovable as a stone," Pip vowed, her eyes bright at the image of St. Ives on his knees, his hands clasped before him as he implored her to accept his escort.

"Oh, no!" Belle protested at once. "You must not be so intractable as all that! You must refuse him, certainly, but you must do it in such a way as to lead him to think you *might* accept at a later date. We wouldn't wish to discourage the poor man."

Pip's smile grew positively wicked. "And you have the gall to accuse *me* of being devious," she said with a delighted chuckle. "Poor St. Ives! If I wasn't so angry with him, I daresay I could almost feel sorry for him. But only almost. Something tells me I shall enjoy leading the viscount a merry chase. In fact, I find I'm rather looking forward to the experience!"

They were due to appear at Almack's that evening, and while Pip was adding the finishing touches to her simple toilet, the maid appeared carrying a small gilded box. "For you, miss," she said importantly, curtseying as she handed it to Pip. "The lad what delivered it said you was to open it at once."

Pip's eyebrows climbed in surprise as she broke off the gold ribbon and lifted the lid, exposing a corsage of creamy white roses. More than a little intrigued, she lifted the flowers from their satiny bed, inhaling their potent fragrance as she read the accompanying note.

My dear Miss Lambert, she read aloud

I know you usually eschew such items of personal adornment, but when I saw these roses in my garden I simply couldn't resist the urge to send them to you. I would deem it a great favor if you would wear them for me this evening. I would also be greatly flattered if you would grant me the honor of a dance.

Yours,

Alexander St. Ives.

"Oh, miss, flowers from a lord!" The maid clasped her hands together in delight. "Have you ever seen the like?"

"Indeed, Alice, I have not," Pip said ruefully, stroking the rose's velvety petals with the tip of her finger. Even though she knew the flowers were but a part of the viscount's campaign to win the wretched bet, she couldn't help but be touched. No man had ever sent her flowers, she mused, and a traitorous part of her took a feminine delight in the exquisite gift.

"You'll wear them, of course, 'twould be rude not to," Alice said decisively, plucking the blossoms from Pip's hand and holding them against her mistress's plain evening gown. She studied the affect a few moments before uttering a politic, "Oh dear."

Pip gazed at her reflection in the glass. "Yes, it does look somewhat ludicrous, does it not?" she said, her spirits drooping at the sight of the stunning roses lying against the dull gray satin of her gown. "Oh, well. I'll simply thank his lordship for the flowers, and—"

"What about one of your other gowns, miss?" Alice interrupted, turning toward the cedar wardrobe. "Mayhap one of them would show them roses to better advantage."

Pip mentally reviewed the contents of her closet, wincing at the thought of what the maid would find. "Don't bother, Alice," she said quickly, "I am sure what I have on is fine. I have never cared a fig for my appearance, you know."

"Indeed, miss, and mighty odd I have thought it," Alice agreed, picking through the dull gray, brown, and blue gowns. "You're a lady, after all, and 'tis only right that you . . . ah, I thought I remembered seeing this." She extracted a gown covered with a thin covering of protective muslin and held it up triumphantly. "There, the very thing I was looking for."

Pip rose from her brocade-covered stool and hurried to the maid's side just as Alice removed the muslin, exposing a stunning gown of emerald silk. "Where did it come from?" Pip demanded, reaching out a tentative finger to stroke the soft material. "I don't recall buying this."

"Your aunt ordered it, miss," Alice explained, examining the gown for any disfiguring wrinkles or spots. "She thought you ought to have something more colorful than them widow's weeds you're always wearing."

Pip was too stunned by the gown's beauty to object to Alice's impertinence. In all her life, she had never seen anything half so lovely, and she would not have been human had she been able to resist it. "It is beautiful," she said, already imagining herself in the stunning gown, smiling up at St. Ives as he gazed at her in stunned amazement. The frivolous image instantly restored her common sense, and she turned away with a scowl.

"You may return the gown, Alice," she said decisively. "The dress I have on is fine, and—"

"The gown you have on would put a governess to the blush," Alice spoke with the blunt familiarity of a valued family retainer, "and I'd be doing you no favors by saying otherwise. Now, sit yourself back down on that stool, and leave everything to me. I'll not have you shaming this family by snubbing his lordship's fine gift."

"Really, Alice, you forget yourself. I—"

"Sit!"

Pip's mouth dropped at the command. She'd always prided herself on her independent nature, but she knew that there were times when even she occasionally had to bend to another's will. Apparently this was one of those occasions. Swallowing her angry retort, she resumed her seat, meekly submitting herself to Alice's knowing ministrations.

He shouldn't have done it, Alex decided, his eyes hooded as he scanned the crowd for Miss Lambert. He shouldn't have sent her those wretched roses. He'd known from the start that she wasn't the sort of female to have her head turned by flowers and the like, but as he had said in the note, he'd been unable to resist the impulse to send them to her. They were almost the very same color and texture as her skin—although, of course, he'd been too wise to say anything so intimate.

Blast this wager! How the hell had things grown so damned complicated? He hated lying to Miss Lambert, hated pretending an interest he didn't feel. Or rather, an interest he *did* feel, he admitted savagely. Perhaps that was the problem. He admired Miss Lambert, and to a certain extent he even liked her. Not in a romantic way, of course, but still—

"Good evening to you, St. Ives," Toby drawled, materializing before Alex. "You are looking particularly poetic this evening."

"I beg your pardon?" Alex asked, shifting to one side so that he could still see the Assembly Room.

"Poetic," Toby repeated, gesticulating with his quizzing glass. "Dark and brooding, rather like a dangerous bird of prey."

Alex gave a derisive snort. "Idiot," he muttered, his troubled gaze swinging back toward the room. He hoped the tiresome dandy would take offense and leave, but he had sadly underestimated the depth of Toby's stupidity.

"Not a crow, mind. Such dreadfully common creatures, crows—even if you *are* wearing a black jacket. No, I should liken you to a hawk. A proud raptor of the skies, swift and deadly, soaring above—"

"What the devil are you jabbering about?"

Toby blinked at the irritated roar that burst from Alex. "Well, you, old man," he said, his hands fluttering to his cravat. "You're looking as glum as a penny-a-day mourner, and I was but commenting on it. What is amiss? Wager not going well?"

"Then why the hell didn't you say so?" Alex snarled, ignoring the last part of Toby's explanation. He had no intention of discussing the bet or Miss Lambert with this buffoon. "What was all that nonsense about hawks and crows?"

"They are metaphors, my lord. I have decided to become a poet. That is why I am come to you for assistance."

"Me?" Alex gaped at him, more convinced than ever that he was a Bedlamite. "Good God, Flanders, I know nothing about poetry!"

"Of course not." Toby gave a condescending sniff. "You are a rake, and unable to comprehend the more refined arts."

"Flanders . . ."

" 'Tis the wager, you see," Toby explained eagerly. "A poet's mind may dwell in more airy realms, but our bodies, alas, must live on this earthly plain, and that, to be tediously blunt, requires the ready."

Alex sifted through this mountain of nonsense before arriving at a conclusion. "You mean you have wagered against me?"

"No, your lordship, *on* you." Toby gave him an ingenuous smile. "Much better odds, don't you know."

Alex flushed a dull red. The odds, while improving somewhat, were still heavily in Miss Lambert's favor, and his pride chafed at the thought that people were assuming he would fail. "I appreciate your vote of confidence, Flanders," he said heavily, "but again I must remind you that a gentleman would never wager on a lady."

"Too late for that, your lordship." Toby gave a philosophical shrug. "But in any case I see nothing wrong with a fellow making a quid or two, especially in the pursuit of his muse. And on the subject of pursuit, Reggie and I have hit upon the perfect solution to all our problems."

Alex bit back a curse, mentally raising his hands in surrender. "And what might that be?" he asked, thinking that trying to reason with Flanders was not unlike attempting to converse with a chair. Except, of course, that the chair had more sense.

Toby cast a quick look about him before leaning toward Alex. "Well," he began with a conspiratorial whisper, "even though you've done your best to fix Miss Lambert's interest, 'tis obvious she isn't the least bit taken with your charms."

"Now see here, Flanders—"

"Only to be expected, of course. Chit is a bluestocking, and one can not expect her to reason like a normal female. I am sure any other lady would be more than delighted with your suit."

The condescending words made Alex's jaw tighten in anger. "You are too kind," he muttered sarcastically.

"Not at all." Toby was oblivious to the irony in Alex's deep voice. "Where was I? Ah, yes, since Miss Lambert is uninterested in you as a lover, what is required is a change of tactics. That is why you must take her to Thorn Hill."

"Thorn Hill?" Alex frowned at the name.

"Reggie's country house—that is, his father's country house, since the old tartar is still alive and kicking. You must have heard of it; a charming manor house just outside of Tunbridge Wells—"

"I know where it is, blast it!" Alex interrupted, his mouth tightening in raw fury. "What I want to know is what the hell you mean by suggesting I take Miss Lambert there. If you are hinting I should compromise her—"

"Good heavens, no!" Toby was horrified. "You might be forced to marry her if such were the case."

"Then what do you mean?" It was only by calling on his experience at maintaining control that Alex was able to resist the impulse to pick Toby up by the throat and give him a sound shaking.

"A weekend party, my lord. Reggie's sister is having one next weekend, and I am sure with a little persuasion she could see her way clear to inviting both you and Miss Lambert. Think of the opportunities, sir, away from London and its many distractions. Why, I daresay you could convince her to attend a dozen balls once you've had a *real* chance at wooing her!"

Alex stared at him in surprise. Much as he hated admitting it, the plan had possibilities, especially if it helped separate Miss Lambert from The Golden Icicle. That was another trick he'd learned from Wellington: divide and conquer.

"What makes you think Miss Lambert would accept?" he asked, examining the plan for any potential flaws. "I wasn't aware she was acquainted with Kingsford's family."

"Bosom birds," Toby assured him solemnly. "Lydia and Miss Lambert made their bows together. Certainly she would be more than delighted to accept. Not as if she had anything else to do," he added with a mocking laugh.

Alex didn't know about that. Miss Lambert may not have as lively a social calendar as most ladies of the *ton,* but she did manage to keep herself busy. That had been part of the problem, he decided. It was exceedingly difficult to make up to a lady who was forever hurrying off to one meeting or another. But in the country . . .

"Heavens, there she is now!" Toby's exclamation brought Alex's head jerking up, his eyes automatically searching the crowd for the familiar brown or gray gowns Miss Lambert affected. At first his eyes went past the tall brunette in a green gown, only to flash back seconds later. Even as he was absorbing the transformation in her appearance, Toby was edging away.

"I'd best take my leave," he said, speaking quickly. "No need to make your decision just now. Only think on it, your lordship. 'Twill be best for all; you'll see." And then he fled, disappearing into the crowd as if by magic.

Alex was scarce aware of his leaving. His eyes were riveted to Miss Lambert. He'd always thought her passingly pretty, but in the green gown, his white roses pinned to the heart-shaped bodice, he realized she was far more than that. He had no sooner reached this conclusion than she was standing before him, her eyes filled with laughter as she held her hand out to him.

"Good evening, milord. As you can see, I am wearing your roses," she said, her lips lifted in a teasing smile. "The dance, I fear, is another matter."

"What? Another man has stolen a march on me?" he demanded, scowling with mock ferocity even as he swept her gloved hand to his lips. "Tell me his name that I may demand satisfaction!"

Pip mentally applauded him. 'Twas a pity viscounts didn't tread the boards, she thought mockingly. St. Ives could have given Kean himself lessons on how to act the jealous suitor. "He is a she, and her name is Lady Jersey," she said with forced lightness. "I am afraid she is rather miffed with me."

"Not another letter in the radical press, Miss Lambert?" Alex asked, wondering if he should use his influence to win her a reprieve.

"Nothing so scandalous as all that," Pip assured him, still smiling. "Merely a difference of opinion concerning a certain Miss Julia Dolitan. Belle put her name in for a voucher, and Lady Jersey refused it."

"And you naturally sided with Miss Portham," Alex concluded, shaking his head at her. "You are a brave woman indeed, to defy the lioness in her own den."

"Perhaps I am simply a lover of justice," Pip suggested, unfurling her fan. Alice had unearthed it from the bottom of a drawer and insisted she take it. "Miss Dolitan is an exceptional young lady, and more than deserving of a voucher. I think it petty and small-minded to refuse her one merely because her brother is in trade."

"And you told this to Lady Jersey?"

Pip shrugged her shoulders. "More or less, yes."

Alex grinned widely. "Knowing you, Miss Lambert, those words were 'more,' rather than 'less.' Again, I commend you for your bravery," he said, his eyes resting on her with admiration. He realized he had yet to compliment her on her appearance, and hastened to rectify his mistake.

"May I also be allowed to commend you on your good looks?" he asked, his tone warmly intimate. "You are looking particularly lovely this evening."

To her everlasting shame, Pip felt herself flushing with pleasure at the compliment. Although she'd rather die than admit as much, she'd been a trifle disappointed when he'd failed to comment on her new gown. That she should behave so missishly appalled her, and she retreated behind a half-smile.

"Thank you, your lordship—although to be honest, it is my aunt who is deserving of your praise. She is the one who commissioned this gown for me."

Alex laid his hand on her arm. "It is not your gown that makes you beautiful, Phillipa," he said, his voice deep as he gazed into her eyes. "It is you yourself."

Because his husky words brought her such pleasure, Pip turned her head to scan the room. "I wonder what is keeping Belle," she said in an overly bright voice. "She promised me most faithfully she would be here, and 'tis not like her to break her word."

"Perhaps Lady Jersey has barred the door against her?" Alex suggested, reluctantly accepting the change of conversation. He knew she thought he had been flattering her, but the truth was he had meant every word. The realization was daunting.

"Ha! As if she would dare!" Pip gave a light laugh at the thought. "No, more likely there is a problem with one of her ladies. I am sure she will be here when she can."

They continued chatting for several more minutes before Alex said, "As you cannot dance, Miss Lambert, would you care to take a turn about the room with me? I do not know about you, but if I do not move soon, I fear I may begin to take root like our poor friend there," and he nodded at a wilted palm sitting forlornly in the corner.

The humorous image his bantering words conjured brought a ready laugh to Pip's lips. "Well, we certainly wouldn't want *that*," she said, taking his proffered arm as they began walking about the crowded room. It was just as well she knew about the wager, she thought as she nodded at an acquaintance, else she might have been taken in by the viscount's flirtatious ways. As she had already observed to Belle, he could be a devastatingly charming man.

As they continued their circumambulation of the room, Alex was painfully aware of the stares they were drawing. People gaped at them in open-mouthed astonishment. He could almost hear the speculative conversations being conducted behind their cupped hands and feathered fans. Perhaps now the odds might turn in his favor, he thought, then winced with remorse that he should be so lacking in personal honor.

He was still brooding on the matter when he caught the word "wager" being uttered by a plump man in a badly cut jacket. He jerked in reaction and cast a quick glance at Miss Lambert. She seemed not to have noticed, but he realized the futility of keeping the bet secret from her. And if she were ever to learn of it . . .

"I have been thinking, Miss Lambert," he said abruptly, deciding he had procrastinated long enough, "and I believe I may know of a way to help your friend Miss Dolitan."

"Oh? And pray, your lordship, what might that be?" Pip answered, her eyes on an older woman who was staring at her and Lord St. Ives with undisguised curiosity. If the lady leaned over any further she would tumble headfirst into the orgeat bowl, she mused, her eyes gleaming with silent laughter.

"Well." Alex cleared his throat, annoyed to discover he was as nervous as a callow youth about to approach his first woman. "You must know that Prinny ... er ... His Royal Highness, is a particular friend of Lady Jersey's. I am sure if he asked the countess, she would be delighted to extend a voucher to the young lady in question."

His words brought Pip crashing down to earth with a vengeance. She'd been enjoying herself so much that she'd actually forgotten the wretched wager. Quickly masking her reaction, she managed a vague smile.

"I am sure she would," she said with what she hoped was a sophisticated laugh. "But unfortunately I do not know the prince, and it is unlikely I should ever have the opportunity to ask him to intercede on Miss Dolitan's behalf."

Here was the opportunity he had been waiting for, but rather than the triumph he had been expecting to feel, Alex was aware of a sense of disappointment. Nevertheless he pressed on, determined to put this unpleasant mess behind him once and for all. "As it happens I am personally acquainted with the regent," he said carefully. "In fact, I have received an invitation to attend his ball at Carlton House. Perhaps you would care to attend with me so that I might introduce you?"

To give the wretch his due, Pip had to admit he made his invitation seem a genuine one. Indeed, if she hadn't known any better, she would have sworn he sounded nervous—almost as if he feared she would refuse him. As perhaps he did, she decided cynically. Remembering Belle's careful instructions, she turned to him with a look of genuine regret on her face.

"That is very kind of you, your lordship," she said in

her sweetest voice, "but I am sure we need not bother his highness with so trifling a matter. Belle and I are not without resources, and I am confident we may yet triumph over Lady Jersey and her crowd."

"I am sure you shall, Miss Lambert," Alex protested, scarce believing she had actually refused him. "But the fact remains that a royal patron could only help your friend. You—"

"Oh look, there is Belle now," Pip interrupted, mentally thanking her friend for her timely arrival. She turned to St. Ives and gave him another smile.

"Thank you once again for your generous offer," she said, laying a hand on his arm, "but as I say, there really is no need. Perhaps some other time?"

Alex took his disappointment like a man. "Yes, perhaps some other time," he said stoically, lifting her hand to his lips for a brief kiss. "Good evening to you, then."

He watched silently as she threaded her way through the maze of people to the corner where Miss Portham was standing. So much for that plan, he thought, his lips thinning in anger. Clearly, more desperate actions were indicated. He turned away and began searching for Toby.

He found the younger man in the card room languidly enjoying a game of whist. Ignoring Toby's petulant complaints, he dragged him away from the table and led him to a secluded corner.

"Were you serious about this weekend party?" he demanded, his eyes hard as he stared down into Toby's flushed face.

"Certainly I was serious," Toby replied, fairly bristling with indignation. "A fellow doesn't joke about so serious a matter as money."

"Good," Alex said grimly. "Because I want you to arrange everything. See that Miss Lambert receives her invitation no later than tomorrow afternoon."

Toby's jaw dropped in astonishment. "But—but—your lordship—"

"Just see to it," Alex interrupted coldly, his mind already on the next battle. "I will take care of everything else."

Six

Pip and Belle shared a celebratory cup of tea the next afternoon, and Belle listened in wry amusement as Pip crowed over her defeat of the viscount.

"You should have seen his face." She laughed, her green eyes dancing as she recalled the frustration on St. Ives's handsome features. "He looked so annoyed I vow I thought he would pop!"

Belle smiled slightly. "Well, it certainly sounds as if you handled the initial offer most effectively," she said, lifting her cup in a mocking salute. "Will there be others, do you think?"

"Oh, undoubtedly; his lordship is nothing if not tenacious," Pip assured her with an impish smile. "Would you care to hear how I intend handling those?"

They spent the next several minutes discussing various stratagems until the maid appeared carrying a note for Pip. Remembering the roses St. Ives had sent her yesterday, she eagerly broke the wax circlet sealing the letter and scanned its contents.

"What on earth?" she said, her brows meeting in puzzlement.

"What is it?" Belle attempted to get a peek at the missive.

"It is from Lydia Kingsford," Pip answered, handing her the letter. "She has invited me to her home for next weekend."

Belle read the letter, her lips curving in a derisive smile. "She does have an interesting way of issuing an invitation, doesn't she? 'We shall expect you and your aunt at seven o'clock.' " Almost as if your acceptance is a foregone conclusion."

"Well, if that is how she feels, then she is in for a sore disappointment," Pip grumbled, retrieving the letter and rereading it with a scowl. "I could never tolerate her above half, and until now I thought the feeling was reciprocated. I cannot imagine why she would wish to invite me."

"I wonder . . ."

"What?" Pip glanced up at the speculative note in Belle's voice.

"Lydia is related to Reginald Kingsford, is she not?"

"His sister," Pip agreed, her nose wrinkling in distaste. "I could never tolerate him, either. Affected dandy."

"It was Reginald who insisted St. Ives accept the bet," Belle continued, looking thoughtful.

Pip's eyes grew wide with understanding. "Ah, then you think the wager is responsible for Lydia's sudden desire for my company?"

"I should think it most likely, especially if Kingsford wagered *against* your accepting the viscount's invitation. 'Tis obvious he means to hedge his bet by putting some distance between you."

"How extraordinary," Pip marveled, torn between admiration and annoyance. "I would never have thought him capable of such cunning. Evidently I have sadly underestimated the wretch."

"Then you mean to refuse?"

Pip fluttered her eyelashes in an attempt at coyness. "But of course," she simpered. "You must know I could not bear to be parted from my beau."

Belle was still chuckling at this when the maid returned to announce Lord St. Ives had called and was asking to see her.

"This appears to be my day for visitors," Pip turned to Belle, taking care to hide her pleasure at the unexpected news. "And here I am without my aunt to lend me countenance. Would you care to stay and act as my duenna?"

"It would be my pleasure," Belle replied with alacrity, her golden eyes sparkling with sudden interest. "I've not had that many opportunities to discourse with his lordship, and there are several things I should like to learn. Do you know his position on the Catholic question?"

"No, but you can always ask him," Pip murmured, her lips curving in a wicked smile. "In fact, I should like to see how you manage to work it into the conversation!"

In the hallway a frustrated Alex hastily revised his battle plans. Learning Miss Portham was with Miss Lambert came as no surprise, considering the time the two spent in each other's company, but it was a complication he would have preferred to avoid. There was something about the self-possessed beauty he found unnerving, and the thought of making his appeal in front of her was more than a little disconcerting. Still, he supposed it could not be helped, and Golden Icicle or nay, he would do whatever it took to convince Miss Lambert to accept the Kingsford invitation.

None of these dark thoughts was evident as he was escorted to the parlor where the ladies were waiting to receive him. After dispensing with the necessary small talk, he got down to the reason for his visit, having deduced that the direct approach was the best way of handling Miss Lambert.

"I was wondering, ma'am, if you have received your invitation to the Kingsfords' weekend party?" he asked casually, knowing full well that the invitation had been delivered by the Kingsfords' footman less than half an hour ago.

Pip and Belle exchanged startled looks. "As a matter of fact, I have," she admitted, her tone cautious as she regarded him. "We were discussing it just as you arrived."

"Have you decided whether or not you will be going?" Alex pressed, his face expressing indifference as he leaned back in his chair. "I am only asking, you see, to determine whether or not I shall also be attending."

There was another exchange of stunned looks. "You were also invited?" Pip asked, making no attempt to mask her surprise. So much for their theory concerning Kingsford's motives, she thought with a wry smile.

"Yes, and I own to being of two minds as to whether or not I shall accept," he admitted with deceptive coolness. "I am not so very well acquainted with Kingsford, and weekend parties do have a tendency to be monstrously dull. Still, if you are to be there I may be persuaded to put in an appearance. I daresay you can be counted upon to liven up any gathering. Do you not agree, Miss Portham?" His brilliant blue eyes cut to Belle's face.

Pip was treated to the rare spectacle of seeing her poised friend flushing like a schoolgirl. "I . . . oh yes, your lordship, to be sure," Belle stammered, her eyes flashing to Pip with a look of almost desperation. "Merry as a cricket, that is our Phillipa."

Pip could only stare to hear herself so described, but before she could demand an explanation Belle added, "Now don't twit his lordship, my dear," she said in a bright voice, quite unlike her usual cool tone. "You know very well you were only just saying you could not wait to see your dear friend Lydia again."

Pip continued staring at Belle, certain her poor friend was suffering from an attack of the vapors. It was the only thing she could think of that would explain her extraordinary behavior. When Belle began jerking her head to one side and rolling her eyes, she was con-

vinced something was seriously amiss. Ignoring the viscount's presence, she rushed to her side.

"Belle, are you all right?" she demanded, anxiously
studying her face. "Is it another headache?"

"What?" Belle stared at her and then said, "Oh . . .
oh yes! My head!" She laid a hand to her forehead and
turned to St. Ives with a wan smile. "If your lordship
will excuse us but for one moment . . ."

"Certainly." Alex was on his feet, trying to decide
what the deuce was going on. He wasn't so green as to
be taken in by Miss Portham's dramatics; it was obvious she wanted to get Miss Lambert off to herself for
a private coze. It was equally obvious that she wanted
her to accept the Kingsfords' invitation. Since that also
fit in with his own designs, he decided to play along.

"I will go and fetch the housekeeper," he said, assuming an appropriately concerned demeanor. "Unless
you think a physician ought to be summoned?"

"Yes!"

"No!"

Pip and Belle glared at each other and then Belle
turned to the viscount. "If you would be so good as to
ask Mrs. Thornton if she has any laudanum, I should be
most grateful," she said with great dignity. "I do hate to
be such a bother, but I fear I am a slave to these
wretched headaches."

"I understand entirely, Miss Portham," he said, executing a deep bow. "I shall return in a few minutes."
And he hurried out of the room, closing the door behind
him.

The moment they were alone Belle gave Pip a shove
of annoyance. "Honestly, Pip, how can you be such a
gudgeon?" she demanded in a thoroughly exasperated
voice. "You must know perfectly well there is nothing
wrong with me!"

"No, I did not know it!" Pip denied, her concern giving way to indignation. "Not with you rolling your eyes

and behaving like some simpering booby! What was I to think but that you had taken sick?"

"You might have thought that I wanted you to accept the Kingsfords' invitation," Belle grumbled. "It is the perfect opportunity for you to be alone with St. Ives."

"Why should I want to be alone with him?" Pip snapped in exasperation. "*You* are the one so set to marry him!"

"Yes, but *you* are the one who was invited to Thorn Hill," Belle pointed out, with that maddening calm for which she was infamous.

Pip tumbled to her meaning at once, and the scowl on her face grew pronounced. "Belle—" she began, suddenly determined to put an end to this nonsense once and for all, "I really do not think—"

"You promised you would help," Belle interrupted softly, her amber eyes reproachful. "You must know I am counting upon you."

Pip closed her eyes and muttered a most unladylike sentiment. Belle had just hit her in her most vulnerable spot, and even though she knew full well it had been a calculated thrust, she was unable to do anything other than agree. Still, she was hanged if she would allow Belle to have things totally her way.

"What about the wager?" she asked, opening her eyes and giving Belle a resigned look. "You realize that is the only reason St. Ives wants me to accept this stupid invitation?"

"Of course." Belle looked indignant that Pip would think her so lacking in gray matter. "But as you yourself have said, what does it matter, so long as the wager also serves our purposes?"

"Things could turn awkward," Pip warned, determined to go down fighting. "The viscount is certain to be annoyed when I keep refusing his invitations to the prince's ball, and I really do not feel like putting up with a sulky peer for two entire days."

"Let him sulk," Belle advised with a negligent shrug.

"Besides, what can he do? He can hardly lock you in a room and force you to accept him."

"That is so," Pip agreed, smiling at the image of the dignified St. Ives shutting her in a dungeon like the villain in a Minerva novel.

"Then you'll tell him you shall be attending the Kingsfords' party?" Belle studied her hopefully.

"I'll tell him I am considering it," Pip said, compromising. "After all, Aunt was invited as well, and I can hardly accept for us both until I know her feelings in the matter."

"She'll accept." Belle gave a wise nod. "You must know that it has been her greatest desire to see you safely wed since she came to live with you. This weekend party will seem a godsend to her, and she'd accept even if it meant giving up tea with the queen."

Pip was all too aware of her aunt's matchmaking dreams. "If she expects me to get married merely because of a weekend party, then she is even more birdwitted than I thought," she answered with a scowl. "I'll not marry anyone, even if they were to shut me up in the Tower of London!"

To her surprise Belle began laughing. "Do you know, I think it is a great pity Lydia Kingsford didn't invite me," she said, her eyes dancing with sudden mischief. "In the event his lordship didn't come up to scratch, I could always have arranged to have myself shut up in a room with him. Then he would have no choice but to marry me."

Pip was shocked to her toes that Belle would contemplate anything so devious. "You wouldn't—"

"Of course not, silly!" Belle shook her head at her. "I was only funning. Now hush, I think I hear St. Ives returning," and she lay back in her chair, closing her eyes as if in excruciating pain.

As Belle had predicted, Mrs. Beachton was delighted at the prospect of attending a weekend party in the country, especially when she learned Lord St. Ives would also be in attendance. Learning they would be making the short journey to Tunbridge Wells in his lordship's carriage, however, sent her into alt.

"He's been most singular in his attentions, do you not think?" she commented happily as she and Pip shared a glass of sherry before setting out for the evening. "Congratulations, my dearest love, I am sure you shall make a lovely bride!"

"Nonsense, Aunt Morwenna," Pip denied, feeling somewhat traitorous for raising her poor aunt's hopes. "He is just being kind, that is all."

"And I suppose he was just being 'kind' when he sent you those lovely roses, hm?" Mrs. Beachton asked, arching her eyebrows in a knowing way. "Don't play coy with me, Phillipa, 'tis plain you have made a conquest of the viscount. How proud your father would be if he knew!"

Pip stiffened at the pain that lashed through her. "I do not know about that, Aunt, but I daresay he would have been highly astonished," she said, and laughed bitterly. "He had given up all hope that I would ever prove a dutiful daughter and marry as I was bid."

There was an uncomfortable silence, but before Pip could apologize for her outburst, Mrs. Beachton was changing the subject. "You will never guess who is back in town, my dear," she said with assumed brightness. "Lord Colford! I saw him with my very own eyes, else I would never have believed it."

"Really?" Because she felt so guilty at having upset her aunt, Pip feigned an interest she did not feel. "I thought he had retired to the country to see to his estates."

"That is the story he put about," Mrs. Beachton allowed with a smirk, "but naturally no one *really* believed it. Everyone knows he left after he and . . . er . . . a certain party all but came to blows over some pretty opera dancer."

Her aunt's stammer brought a sudden grin to Pip's face. "It is too late to wrap it all in clean linen, ma'am," she admonished, wagging a playful finger. "You have already let slip that it was Lord St. Ives who was involved in the scandal. Indeed, I am shocked you would allow me to speak to such a rake, let alone marry him!"

Mrs. Beachton gave her a knowing look. "All men of St. Ives's class have mistresses," she told her in the patient tones of a long-suffering parent. "It would look deuced odd if they did not. It is how a gentleman conducts himself after the marriage that is important."

"And how do you think his lordship would conduct himself?" Pip teased, and was surprised when her aunt took the question seriously.

"I think," she said carefully, "that his lordship could be counted upon to honor his marriage vows and keep himself wholly unto his wife. He is a man one could trust without reservation, for he is a man who would always keep his word."

Her answer shocked Pip, even as she found herself in total agreement. St. Ives was a man of impeccable honor, even if he was involved in this foolish wager, and she knew instinctively that he would never betray the woman he married. In fact, she realized with a sinking sensation, he would make a perfectly wonderful husband. Provided, of course, that one desired such a troublesome creature—which, she told herself firmly, naturally *she* did not.

". . . so funny," her aunt concluded with a laugh. "Do you not agree, Phillipa?"

Pip gave a start, realizing that she had missed most of the other lady's conversation. Rather than admitting as much and asking her aunt to repeat herself, she said, "Yes, Aunt, I most certainly do."

"Well, that is the way with these rakes; the wilder they are, the heavier they tend to come down upon their children," Mrs. Beachton said, taking another sip of sherry. "Not that Toby is Colford's son, thank God, but when a man is thirty-four and still unmarried, one must naturally regard his nearest male relative as his heir. Still, I cannot help but think it hypocritical of Colford to ring a peal over Toby's head for becoming involved in a scandal with St. Ives when he himself did the very same thing less than two months ago."

Pip choked on the sip of sweet wine she had just taken. "The viscount is involved in a scandal?" she gasped, horrified that her aunt might have inadvertently learned of the bet.

"Well, it is nothing horribly scandalous," her aunt hastened to assure her, obviously fearing she would take the viscount into dislike. "Merely something about a wager of some kind."

Pip set her glass on a side table with undue care. "What sort of wager?" she asked, mentally steeling herself for the worst.

Mrs. Beachton looked troubled. "I do not know," she admitted with a frown. "It is really the oddest thing. The moment I catch even a whisper of it the speaker immediately clamps his mouth shut or changes the conversation. It is almost as if I am being kept deliberately in ignorance of the details. Even my oldest friends will not tell me anything."

Pip uttered a silent prayer that society had sufficient scruples to spare the older woman's feelings. "That is probably because they themselves do not know," she said with a strained laugh. "I know *I* haven't heard so much as a whisper about any wager."

Mrs. Beachton gave a wry chuckle. "And since when have you paid society tattle the slightest mind?" she teased, giving Pip's hand a fond pat. "I daresay you wouldn't even notice if it was *you* they were whispering about!"

Pip smiled thinly and reached for her glass. "Oh, I just might, Aunt," she said, taking a deep sip. "I just might."

* * *

"A fine job you did of watching the pup! I'd have done better leaving him with a Covent Garden abbess."

"Don't hurl accusations at me, Colford, 'tis I who by rights ought to be raging at you," Alex replied, his eyes gleaming with amusement as he faced his longtime friend. He'd arrived home from Miss Lambert's to find the earl waiting for him, and the other man wasted little time before letting his displeasure be fully known.

"And why is that?" Marcus Colford demanded, still annoyed. "I told you the lad was an idiot."

"Yes, but you failed to tell me he was a malicious idiot," Alex pointed out, hiding a smile at the sight of Marcus scolding him like an outraged papa. "You know damned well this whole fiasco is his fault, every bit of it. Now cut line and tell me the real reason you are here. It cannot be just to rescue your cousin from my evil clutches, although I shall be eternally grateful if you do so. The boy's charm wears thin upon close acquaintance."

Lord Colford's lips tightened, but in another moment he was joining Alex in laughter. "Bastard," he said, throwing himself onto one of the wing chairs facing the fireplace. "I suppose it is no less than I deserve. Leaving Toby in your care was a harebrained thing to do."

"My sentiments exactly," Alex agreed amiably. "Why the hell did you do it?"

Marcus contemplated the toe of his shining Hessians with a frown. "Because I couldn't figure out a way to drag him back with me, and there was no way I could remain in town when things were in such a damned coil at home."

"Any improvement?" Alex asked sympathetically, having already been brought into the earl's confidence.

"Some." Marcus's gray eyes were bitter. "I had to sell off my estates outside of Brampton and lease some other property near Burroughton, but I think I have satisfied the last of my father's creditors, thank God."

Alex held his glass of wine up to the light. "If you have need of any monies—" he began carefully, only to be interrupted by Marcus.

"No, thank you." The earl tempered his refusal with a warm smile. "I am not so sunk that I must leech off my friends. Although if you know any available heiress, you might want to introduce me to her. A marriage of convenience would prove the answer to all my prayers just now."

"As a matter of fact, there is someone," Alex said, thinking of Miss Portham. "Worth a half-million, they say, and quite a beauty in the bargain. I could arrange an introduction."

"If you are talking about Arabella Portham, you needn't bother," Marcus replied, a devilish smile lifting the corners of his mouth. "The ... er ... lady and I already know each other."

"Oh?"

"Not like that." Marcus recognized the speculative note in Alex's voice. "We are enemies, not lovers."

"And how did this come about?" Alex was intrigued to think of the haughty Miss Portham unbending enough to quarrel with anyone.

"It was years ago." Marcus thrust a careless hand through his russet-colored hair. "I'd had enough brandy to make me bold enough to try and steal a kiss—and was almost frozen to death for my pains. When she slapped my face I called her The Golden Icicle, and she has scarce had a civil word to say to me since."

"Then perhaps I shan't introduce you after all," Alex drawled, hiding a grin at the thought of a younger Marcus wrestling with the icy blond on a moonlit balcony.

"As I said, there is no need. That is another reason I am so hipped about this damned wager. Miss Lambert is Miss Portham's closest friend, and when she learns of it you may be very sure she will be quick to lay the blame on my doorstep."

"That hardly seems fair, considering you were tucked away in the Cotswolds at the time." Alex frowned. "How can she blame you?"

"I don't know, but she will, mark my words," Marcus predicted glumly. "And the last thing I need just now is another enemy. Damn Toby's eyes! A pity he is too big for caning."

"If you hold him, I'll get the cane," Alex offered with a feral smile. "Besides, what about that snake Kingsford? He's far more to blame than your block-headed cousin. I'm more than certain he's the one who spread news of the bet to the clubs."

"As am I—but Kingsford, thankfully, is not my responsibility."

"No, but he may just end up being mine."

Alex's calm announcement made Marcus's eyes narrow in concern. "If you are talking about a duel—" he warned in a low voice.

"Nothing so dramatic." Alex held up a placating hand. "I just may find it necessary to have a word with the lad, that is all. I do not trust him."

"Then why the devil are you attending his weekend party?" Marcus demanded, his brows gathering in a frown.

"Because I want this damned wager ended!" Alex snapped, leaning forward in his chair. "And the best way I can do that is to get Miss Lambert to accompany me to the prince's ball! She's already refused me once, but perhaps in the country and away from all the distractions I can convince her to change her mind. It is my only choice."

"There *is* another way, you know," Marcus suggested carefully.

"If you're going to suggest I forfeit the wager, I shouldn't bother." Alex gave him an angry look. "I've already thought it over and decided against it. I should never live it down, and I doubt it would end the gossip, anyway."

"Add to it, more like," Marcus said in agreement. "No, what I had in mind was something a trifle less self-sacrificing."

"What?"

"Tell her the truth and throw yourself on her tender mercies. I know Miss Lambert, and for all she can cut a man to ribbons with that tongue of hers, she is a nice enough female. Once she knows the truth of the wager, I am sure she can be persuaded to help you."

"But that would be cheating!"

"Don't be so bloody noble, St. Ives." Marcus laughed in response to Alex's outraged tones. "What makes you think Kingsford wouldn't do exactly the same thing if the situation was reversed? There is nothing in the wager that says she must remain in ignorance of the bet, is there?"

"No," Alex admitted, tempted against his will. It would solve everything, he thought, turning it over in his mind. And if she did accept and agree to help him, then it would mean she didn't totally hate him. On the other hand, if he did tell her and she refused . . .

"No," he said, his jaw firming with resolve. "No. I prefer to hold my tongue and take my chances honestly."

"You may lose," Marcus cautioned in a soft voice. "Are you prepared to face the tattle *that* could cause?"

"There will be talk regardless." Alex shrugged his shoulders. "This way, at least I will have the satisfaction of knowing I did my best. If I learned anything in the army, it was that not all battles end in victory."

"A most pragmatic philosophy," Marcus approved, "but in a battle at least both sides know they are fighting; sometimes they may even know why. Will Miss Lambert have that luxury?"

Alex's eyes flashed in frustration. "Damn it, Marcus, what else would you have me do?"

"Nothing." Marcus sent him an apologetic look. "You are indeed in a quandary, my friend. No matter what you do, your honor—and possibly that of Miss Lambert's—will suffer."

"I know that," Alex said in a voice filled with quiet anguish. "That is why this weekend party is so important. But regardless of the outcome, I am determined to end matters then and there. If she refuses me, I will go back to London and publicly admit defeat."

"And if she accepts?"

"Then I'll escort her to the ball and afterwards confess all," Alex replied with a bitter laugh. "Not the actions of a gentleman, I grant you, but then what other choice have I? As you said, regardless of what I do, we will suffer the consequences, and there is nothing I can do that will alter that. Nothing."

Seven

Pip spent the next week frantically preparing for the visit. Realizing that not even she could arrive at Thorn Hill "looking no better than a poor parson's daughter"—to quote Belle—she dashed off to Bond Street to throw herself on Madam Duvall's tender mercies. Closing her eyes to the expense, she ordered up an entire wardrobe, paying double the usual price to insure all would be ready in time. As they would be making the journey in the viscount's carriage, she also ordered a traveling outfit of mulberry velvet, telling herself she was only doing this so as not to disgrace her aunt.

The day before they were to leave, she was sitting in the garden reading when a shadow fell across her. Expecting to see her aunt, she waited until she'd finished the paragraph she was reading before casually glancing up. Her eyes widened when she saw St. Ives standing before her. Without speaking he reached out and plucked the slim volume from her fingers, his lips lifting in a rueful grin at the title stamped into the maroon leather.

"Wollstonecraft," he murmured, his dark blue eyes sparkling with amusement as he glanced down at her. "I might have known."

Pip flushed at the teasing words and snatched the book back, cradling it protectively against her chest. "A most intelligent and insightful lady," she retorted, ignoring the racing of her heart. "I particularly agree with her observation that most men are unspeakable tyrants."

Rather than debating the point, he merely smiled, enjoying the sight of the sunlight spilling over her. She was wearing a fashionable gown of green and gold striped gauze, and although her hair was pulled back in her customary prim chignon, a few tendrils had escaped to curl attractively about her flushed face. He toyed with the idea of reaching out to brush one of the soft curls back into place, and was surprised at the pleasure the thought gave him.

"Your aunt sent me to bring you in for tea," he said, reminding himself of the reason he had come. "But first, I am hoping you will show me your garden. They are such a rarity in London."

Pip knew she ought to refuse, but she thrust the notion aside. It wasn't as if she was a sweet young deb who must zealously guard her reputation, she reminded herself sternly. Besides, what possible harm could come from an innocent stroll in a sunlight garden? "I had it designed for my aunt," she said, accepting his arm as she rose to her feet. "When she came to live with me, she mentioned that one of the things she missed most in her travels with my uncle was a good English garden."

"I know well what she means," Alex murmured in a distracted voice, pausing to admire a late-blooming daffodil. "Many was the time I would have gladly exchanged the most exotic blooms in Portugal for one single English rose."

Pip hid her surprise at his comment, and at the bleak look that stole across his face. She realized this was the first time he had mentioned his years in the army, and she was suddenly anxious to learn more of him. "Were you posted on the peninsula very long, your lordship?" she asked, slanting him a curious look.

If anything, his expression grew even more bleak as he recalled the death and horror he had seen. "Aye," he said softly, "long indeed."

Pip didn't know what to say. She heard the pain in his voice and wanted more than anything to comfort him. Her fingers tightened on his arm, drawing him to a halt beside her. "Was it so very bad?" she asked gently, raising her eyes to study his face.

Alex stared down into her compassionate green eyes. "At times it was all right," he admitted, unable to hold back the truth. "But there were other times when it was hell on earth."

As if of its own volition her hand stole up to touch the rigid line of his jaw. "I am sorry, Alex," she said, his given name slipping unbidden from her lips. "I am so very sorry."

Alex swallowed at the feel of her fingers softly brushing his flesh. He was aware of the sweet smell of her perfume and the softness of her body standing close to his, and he ached to pull her close. His hands closed convulsively about her narrow waist and his head bent toward hers when a voice called out, shattering the sensual spell enveloping them.

"Phillipa! Your lordship! Where are you? The tea is getting cold!"

He jerked at the intrusive sound and took a quick step backwards, his breath coming out in a ragged sigh of disappointment. Without a word he offered Phillipa his arm, and they quietly made their way back to the portico where Mrs. Beachton was waiting for them.

"There you are," she gushed, giving them a maternal smile. "I was beginning to think you had gotten lost!"

"We were but discussing literature, Aunt Morwenna," Pip said calmly, struggling for composure. "It seems his lordship takes a rather dim view of my tastes."

"I'd hardly call that drivel of Wollstonecraft's 'literature,' Miss Lambert," Alex said, easily following her lead.

"Wollstonecraft!" Mrs. Beachton cringed as she led them to the parlor, where a lavish tea had been laid out.

"Never say you have been reading that . . . that woman!"

"Indeed I have." Pip took her place behind the tea cart and began dispensing the hot beverage. She realized her hand was still shaking, and prayed no one would notice. But when she handed Alex—as she now thought of him—his cup, their eyes met and a look of silent understanding flowed between them. Anxious to cover her reaction, she hastily glanced away and began chatting aimlessly.

"I must own I am surprised to see you, sir," she said, her eyes locked on her teacup. "We've not seen you in several days, and I was beginning to think you had set out for Tunbridge Wells without us."

"Never. In fact I am quite looking forward to the journey," Alex assured her smoothly. "But I fear my duties have prevented me from calling upon you—or anyone else, for that matter."

"Your parliamentary duties, sir?" She did glance up at that, her head tipped coquettishly to one side as she challenged him.

He smiled in appreciation. "No, although I am sure it will cast me in your black books for admitting as much. Rather, it is my duties as a lord I was referring to. My steward has written that the housekeeper has run off with the neighbor's French chef, and my household is in chaos. I have spent the past three days interviewing candidates, and I fear I am no closer to resolving the dilemma."

"It seems rather odd that your steward should bother you over so trifling a matter," Pip replied, frowning slightly as she considered his difficulty.

"I agree wholeheartedly, but Jackson, it seems, is of another mind. He feels there is no problem dealing with the estate that is too small not to warrant my immediate attention," Alex said, shrugging his shoulders. "In the meanwhile, the matter will have to wait until I return from the country."

"What you need, your lordship, is a wife," Mrs. Beachton offered, sliding a meaningful look in Pip's direction. "Then you would not be disturbed by such matters."

Pip flushed at her aunt's obvious gambit. "Our housekeeper, Mrs. Carson, has a sister who is also an experienced housekeeper," she said, speaking quickly. "She is between positions at the moment, and Belle had promised to help her. If you would be interested—"

"Say no more, ma'am," Alex interrupted, amused by the adroit way she had handled her aunt's machinations. "Only, send her directly to my house for an interview. If she is good enough to please Miss Portham, I am sure I shall find her more than satisfactory."

"Naturally, if you were married, your *wife* would conduct all interviews," Mrs. Beachton continued doggedly, determined to make her point. It was perfectly plain to her that the viscount was dangling after Phillipa, and if her niece was too foolish to see that, she was not.

"So she would, Mrs. Beachton," Alex agreed, his eyes flicking toward Phillipa. He tried envisioning her in the role of the lady of the manor, shrewdly interrogating prospective candidates, and to his discomfort, the image sprang easily to mind. She would make a formidable viscountess, he decided, and then wondered why the thought did not alarm him as much as it should have. In fact, he found the whole notion rather pleasing . . .

"Dearest Phillipa, so *delightful* to see you again!" Miss Lydia Kingsford greeted Pip with a languid smile, offering her a limp hand to shake. "I am so glad you were able to come—and at the last moment, too. How fortunate you were not otherwise engaged."

"Yes, that was fortunate, was it not?" Pip agreed, thinking that Lydia was every bit as unpleasant as she remembered. It looked to be a long weekend, and her shoulders slumped with weariness. The ride down from London had taken twice as long as anticipated, owing to an accident on the road, and her head was throbbing with pain. She wanted nothing more than to seek her own bed before dinner, but in the meanwhile she had to stand and watch as Lydia brazenly flirted with Alex.

"Ah, Lord St. Ives." Lydia's pale gray eyes rested on Alex's face with obvious interest. "I was *so* pleased when Reggie told me you would be coming. You were so long in responding I thought you meant to refuse!" She pouted enticingly.

"Certainly not, Miss Kingsford," Alex replied with a low bow, hiding his dislike behind a cool facade. "It was kind of you to ask me."

"Nonsense." Lydia gave a throaty laugh, her eyes flicking back to Pip with obvious speculation. "After Reggie told me of meeting you at Almack's ball, I was quite determined that you should attend. I'll *wager* we shall be in for an interesting time, *n'est-ce pas?*"

Alex's dark brows descended in a scowl at Miss Kingsford's play on words. So Kingsford had tattled to his sister as well, he thought, his eyes icing over with displeasure. It was definitely time he had a word with the other man.

Lydia turned her attention to Mrs. Beachton and bade her welcome with a condescending civility that had Pip gnashing her teeth in silent frustration. If she got through the next two days without throttling the other woman it would be a minor miracle, she decided, listening as Lydia was directing them to their rooms.

"I have given you a room in the east wing, next to my cousin," she told Mrs. Beachton with a stiff smile. "She is an elderly lady close to your own age, and I thought perhaps the two of you would enjoy getting to know each other."

"That is most kind of you, Miss Kingsford, thank you," Mrs. Beachton was aware she was being snubbed, but decided it was of no consequence. "Will my niece and I be sharing rooms?"

To Pip's astonishment Lydia laid her hand on her arm. "I hope you do not mind, but I have decided to place her in the room next to mine," she said, flashing Pip a smile that was patently false. "It has been *ages* since we have seen each other, and I am hoping we will have time for a long, comfortable coze!"

"And where will Lord St. Ives be staying?" Mrs. Beachton asked, bending a sapient eye on Alex. She still harbored hopes for a match, but that did not mean she was wholly lost to the practicalities of the situation.

Lydia's gray eyes took on a malicious sparkle. "Why, in the west wing, of course," she said, fairly purring. "Now if you will excuse me, I am afraid I must be seeing to my other duties. The servants will show you to your rooms. We shall be dining at seven."

Pip was conducted to her room by a giggling maid, and the sight of the elegant room came as a pleasant surprise. She wouldn't have put it above Lydia to place her in the smallest, poorest room in the house, but instead she'd been shown to one that was both large and quite lovely. It would have been nice to think she'd misjudged her hostess, but somehow Pip doubted it. Lydia was a shrew; her remark about "wagers" proved that, and if she was being nice to her guest, then she was doing so for a reason. With that thought in mind, Pip began unpacking her bags.

The rest of the afternoon passed in a rather dreary fashion. While Alex toured the stables with Reginald, Pip and her aunt were being shown about Thorn Hill by an annoyingly smug Lydia. More than once Pip found herself biting her tongue as Lydia taunted her; throwing out the words "wager" and "bet" at every conceivable opportunity until Pip was ready to lock her in the priest's hole Lydia had proudly showed them. The only thing that stopped her was the knowledge she need only endure Lydia for another forty-eight hours, and then never see her again. It was almost enough to keep her from boxing Lydia's ears when she "wagered" Pip had never seen a genuine Turner landscape. Almost.

In the stables Alex was faring little better. He'd taken advantage of the situation by reading Reginald a blistering lecture, but the other man seemed oblivious to his cold anger. When he warned the other man what would happen if he didn't control his malicious sister, Reginald merely shrugged.

"It is just Lydia's way, your lordship. Ignore her; I do."

"I've no intention of ignoring her," Alex retorted, his lips thinning with impatience. "Not when she could jeopardize everything. Miss Lambert is far from stupid, you know."

"I don't know about that." Reginald paused to scratch one of his hunters behind its ears. "She ain't tumbled to it yet. How clever can she be if . . . sir!" His words ended in a frightened squawk when Alex grabbed him and threw him against the stable door.

"Let me explain this one more time," Alex enunciated between clenched teeth, his fingers tightening about Kingsford's throat. "No one—*no one*—is to say another word about either Miss Lambert or the wager. Am I making myself clear?"

"P–perfectly, your lordship," Reginald stammered, his hands plucking uselessly at Alex's fingers. "I s–shall see to it at once!"

"See that you do." Alex didn't loosen his grip, but rather tightened it. "And while you're about it, mind your own wagging tongue as well. I still haven't decided whether or not I shall call you out for the damage you've already caused, so I would tread very carefully if I were you."

The threat in Alex's cold voice had Reginald paling in fear. "I–of course, your lordship," he said, attempting to swallow. "A–as you say."

Alex gave him a measuring glare, thinking of the

pleasure it would give him to throttle the miserable little worm. In the end he decided Kingsford wasn't worth it, and took a careful step backwards, his hands dropping to his side.

"Remember what I have said, Kingsford," he said, his eyes holding Reginald's nervous gaze. "Because I have just given you your final warning." He turned and walked away, almost reaching the door before Reginald called out to him.

"Your lordship?"

"What is it?" Over his shoulder, Alex sent him an impatient look.

Reginald moistened his lips with a nervous tongue. "Will–will you be asking Miss Lambert to the prince's ball while you're here?"

Alex gave a heavy sigh. "That *is* why I am here," he reminded him grimly.

"And if she refuses?"

Alex remembered his conversation with Marcus. "Then I will do what I should have done the moment I learned you had spread this tale all over London. I shall go back to town and cover my losses."

Reginald's face grew even more pale, his shoulders drooping despondently. "That," he said unhappily, "is what I was afraid you would say."

As the other guests wouldn't be arriving until late, dinner was an informal affair, and Pip and the others retired soon afterwards. The next morning she rose early and, as the rest of the household was still abed, she decided to go for a ride. It had been years since she'd had such an opportunity, and she was anxious to take advantage of it. Disdaining the offer of the ostler to send one of the grooms with her, she set out on her own to explore the bridle path. She hadn't gotten very far when she heard the sound of approaching hoofbeats and turned to find Alex approaching her at a gallop.

"Good morning, your lordship!" She greeted him with a happy smile, delighting in the soft beauty of the morning and the unexpected chance to converse privately with him. "A lovely day, is it not?"

Rather than responding with a polite smile, his expression was thunderous as he drew up even with her. "What do you mean riding out alone?" he demanded, his dark brows meeting in a scowl. "These paths are unfamiliar to you. What if you had become lost?"

Pip's smile and good mood vanished with the censorious words. "Then I should have found my way back again," she said, her small chin coming up with pride. "Now if you will excuse me, I shall be on my way. 'Tis obvious you would rather be alone." Her hands tightened on the reins as she made as if to ride off.

Alex reached out and grabbed the halter. "Phillipa, wait."

"What?" She sent him a suspicious scowl.

His lips twitched at her hostile expression. "Never give an inch, eh, Phillipa?" he asked, his earlier annoyance vanishing.

"Not if I can help it," she answered warily, not quite trusting his sudden friendliness.

Alex threw back his head and laughed, causing the big gray he was riding to dance nervously. A few deft pulls at the reins stilled the animal, and Alex was still grinning as he released Pip's horse. "Will it help if I admit I shouldn't have snapped at you like that?" he asked, his blue eyes warm in the sunlight. "It was very wrong of me. Wollstonecraft would doubtlessly have been shocked."

Pip blinked, surprised not only by his apology, but also by the sincerity with which he uttered it. She tried reminding herself that he was only making up to her because of the bet, but that did little to stop the glow of happiness spreading through her. She tilted her head to one side, unable to hold back an answering smile.

"Wollstonecraft," she told him with a soft laugh, "would have expected no less. Didn't I tell you she said all men were tyrants?"

"So you did," Alex agreed, his horse falling into step beside her as they continued down the path. "But I hope I am not sunk so low in your estimation as all that."

"Well"—Pip slanted him a mischievous look—"perhaps 'tyrant' is a trifle harsh."

"Thank you, ma'am."

" 'Masterful' is far more accurate. Lord of all you survey, and determined to keep it so."

Alex smiled at her telling description of him. "Again I thank you, ma'am," he said, sending her a devastating smile. "Although I am not quite sure you meant that as a compliment."

Pip's only response was a mysterious smile, and they continued their ride in companionable silence. Every once in awhile she would slide a thoughtful look in his direction, thinking how fine and handsome he looked in his dark blue velvet riding jacket, his black hair tousled by the warm breeze. She remembered the first time she had seen him at Almack's, and wondered again how she and Belle could have selected him for the role of Belle's acquiescent husband. It was more obvious than ever that he would not suit, and this time she was determined to make that clear to Belle. The moment she was back in London she would tell her friend that she would have no part in her silly scheme.

"By the way," Alex said unexpectedly, breaking the silence between them, "I meant to ask, but how is your friend Miss Dolitan? Was Miss Portham able to secure a voucher for her?"

"As a matter of fact, she was," Pip answered easily, grateful for the diversion. "Belle is nothing if not resourceful. She was able to convince the other patronesses that Miss Dolitan would prove a most welcome addition to society."

"And how was she able to do that?"

"By making Julia—that is Miss Dolitan's first name—her ward." Pip smiled to think of the adroit way

Belle had circumvented Lady Jersey. "There is some distant family connection, I believe, and once it became known that Belle herself meant to sponsor her, the objections to Julia's background vanished like wood smoke."

"A brilliant piece of strategy." Alex was more than willing to give Miss Portham her due. "Although I am surprised the patronesses are allowing an unmarried female to act as a sponsor. I thought it was only married ladies who were accorded that honor."

Pip bit her lip, remembering Belle's cool assumption that she would be a married lady by the next Season. "Well, naturally Belle won't be her *real* sponsor," she said, thinking quickly. "I believe her cousin, a Mrs. Larksdale, will be acting in that capacity. But Belle is to be the power behind the throne . . . er . . . if you take my meaning."

"Indeed, I can well imagine Miss Portham in such a role," Alex answered with a laugh. "The lady strikes me as the sort who likes to control things. I pity the poor man she marries."

Pip bristled in instant defense of her friend. "That is not so!" she denied, not altogether truthfully. "How dare you say such a thing!"

Her vehemence surprised Alex. "I meant no offense, Miss Lambert," he assured her sincerely. "I was but making a comment, that is all."

"You know nothing about Belle," Pip continued indignantly. "She wasn't born with that fortune, you know. She didn't inherit until she was almost twelve years old, and her life before that was most unpleasant. Her father died unexpectedly, leaving her and her mother penniless, and they were shifted from relation to relation until her mother, too, died. Belle never even had a new gown of her own until after—"

"Phillipa, I said I was sorry," Alex interrupted, leaning forward in his saddle to grasp her arm. "I told you, I was but making idle conversation."

Pip subsided with a pout, feeling far from mollified. She knew she was being unfair, but Alex's censure of Belle hurt her on an oddly personal level. If he thought Belle managing, what must he think of her? she wondered. Belle at least had her fortune and her beauty to compensate. What did she have? The thought made her shoulders droop in defeat.

Alex saw her unhappiness and could have bitten off his tongue. He knew she was devoted to her friend, and he should have realized she would resent any slur on Miss Portham's character. He wished now he'd never mentioned the matter, but it was too late. Having come this far, he had no choice but to continue.

"This is probably the wrong time to bring this up," he ventured, keeping his voice carefully neutral, "but I had a reason for mentioning Miss Dolitan."

"Really? And what might that reason be?"

He winced at the unwelcoming tone in her voice, but plowed ahead. "To renew my request that you accompany me to the prince's ball. You did say to ask you at some other time," he reminded her when she turned to him with an incredulous expression.

Pip could only gape at him, astounded by his audacity. "You want me to accompany you to Carlton House?" she repeated, annoyed that once again, until this moment, she'd completely forgotten about the wager.

"Very much so," Alex said, faintly surprised to find he meant every word. "I know you have refused me once, but I am hoping you will reconsider. Please?"

Pip was suddenly silent, unsure as to what she should say. Now that she had decided not to encourage Belle's madness a moment longer, she knew there was nothing to prevent her from rudely rejecting his invitation, or even from informing him that she knew all about his infamous wager. Yet somehow, she could not. Perhaps, she realized with a horrified start, because in the deep-

est recesses of her heart she was wishing his invitation
was genuine. Wishing she could say yes . . .

"You make it sound most tempting, your lordship,"
she said, knowing it was the only way. "But I fear I
must decline. Thank you."

Alex's shoulders slumped, not in disappointment but
in relief. That was it, then, he thought, his spirits lifting.
He had done all he could. The matter of the wager was
finally resolved, and he could pursue Phillipa with a
free conscience. The realization made his heart race in
eager anticipation.

Several hours later, she stood before her looking
glass, studying her reflection with a critical eye. The
gown was one of Madame Duvall's newest creations,
and she had to admit it was attractive. Fashioned out of
yellow silk and trimmed with azure ribbons, it clung
lovingly to her rounded breasts before cascading in
graceful folds to her feet. The heart-shaped bodice
dipped low in front, baring her shoulders and upper
arms to what Pip considered a shocking degree. The
family emeralds glittered at her throat and ears, and an
aigrette of brilliants and plumes rested in her dark curls.
Fine feathers for fine birds, she mused, raising a hand
to stroke one of the small plumes.

After picking up her fan, she left the room and went
in search of her aunt. She located the older woman in
the drawing room enjoying a glass of sherry with the
other guests. Pip recognized them as being part of
Lydia and Reginald's circle of friends, and she steeled
herself to endure more of the spiteful cattiness she had
already suffered from Lydia. To her surprise, they were
almost painfully polite to her, and if the conversation
wasn't exactly scintillating, then it was at least innocu-
ous. They were discussing the latest scandal involving
Princess Charlotte when Alex strode into the room, his
eyes going immediately to Pip.

An anticipatory hush fell on the room as he walked

to where she sat, his eyes never leaving her face. When he reached her side, he executed a formal bow, catching her hand and carrying it to his lips. "Miss Lambert," he drawled, his eyes meeting hers as he slowly straightened. "May I be allowed to say how charming you look this evening? That is a lovely gown."

For a moment Pip forgot all about the wager, allowing herself to believe his compliment was as sincere as the admiration in his sapphire-blue eyes. Her cheeks flushed with warm color both at his words and at the feel of his lips on her skin, and in that space of time the rest of the world ceased to exist. Then something— perhaps a snicker from Lydia—recalled her to her senses, and she quickly withdrew her hand from his grasp.

"Your lordship is too kind," she said, seeking refuge behind her fan. "Thank you."

Before Alex could say anything else Lydia gave an unpleasant laugh, her eyes flashing to Pip with obvious enmity. "Yes, I was just about to compliment Miss Lambert on her toilet," she said, her voice dripping with honey. "It is so refreshing to have a guest who feels she need not dress for dinner. Usually they fuss for hours with their appearance while we must wait upon them. But then, as she is such a noted bluestocking, I am sure she never gives such matters a moment's consideration."

There was an uncomfortable silence as all the guests shifted nervously on their chairs. Alex's lips thinned in fury at the woman's ill-mannered cruelty. When they'd returned from their ride, he had gone directly to Kingsford, telling him his offer had been rejected, and it was obvious the treacherous dog had wasted little time in seeking out his bitch of a sister. Evidently Miss Kingsford now considered Phillipa fair game—a mistake that would cost her dearly, he decided, prepared to administer a crushing setdown.

"Oh never." Pip spoke first, managing a light laugh

that concealed the true depths of her fury. "In fact, I have always thought that it is only the most empty-headed of females who bother with such fustian. Do you not agree?"

Lydia's cheeks flushed a bright crimson as she realized, belatedly, that her victim was prepared to fight back. "No," she said tersely, abandoning all pretense of breeding. "I do not."

"Really?" Pip arched her eyebrows in feigned surprise, her eyes resting mockingly on Lydia's gown of cherry-red silk decorated with lavish ribbons and bows. "How odd. From the look of that gown I felt sure you would agree with me."

The silence in the room grew even more pronounced as the guests sat stiff as statues, their gazes locked on their cups of tea. Pip was well aware her behavior was outrageous, but she had taken all of Lydia's spitefulness she was prepared to endure. Deciding she had nothing left to lose, she turned to the man sitting next to her and began quizzing him about the new labor bill.

The topic saw them safely, more or less, through the next hour until dinner was announced. Pip rose with the rest of the guests, her face coolly composed despite her lingering anger. It had never been her intention to cause a public scandal, of course, but she took a grim satisfaction in knowing she'd gotten some of her own back. Perhaps after dinner she—She slammed into Alex who was standing in front of her, blocking her path to the door.

"Miss Lambert," he said, his eyes every bit as cold as his voice as he held out his arm to her. "If you will allow me?"

Pip would have liked to refuse, but she caught the warning scowl her aunt was sending her, and decided she'd created enough havoc for one afternoon. Lifting her chin with defiant pride, she laid her hand on his velvet-clad arm and followed him into the elegant dining room.

Despite the inauspicious beginning, the rest of the evening was surprisingly pleasant. Pip was never one to hold a grudge, and she was even polite to Lydia as she and the other ladies sat in the parlor waiting for the gentlemen to join them for a peaceful session of whist and conversation. Soon the men returned, smelling of cigars and brandy, and this time she was prepared when Alex deliberately sought her out.

"I thought perhaps you might like to walk with me in the gardens," he said, keeping his voice low. "They are said to be quite lovely by moonlight."

Pip was sure they were, and she was equally certain that there would be no end to the speculation if she was so foolish as to accompany him. "I am afraid it is a trifle too cold for me, your lordship," she said, dismissing him with a distant smile.

Rather than accepting his *congé* as she expected, he reached down and grasped her arm, pulling her gently but inexorably to her feet. "I insist, Miss Lambert." He spoke the words with a smile, but that didn't make them any less an order.

Fearful of attracting any more attention, she allowed herself to be led out of the parlor and onto the stone balcony that opened onto the garden. The moment they were outside, however, she pulled free, her eyes snapping with fury as she turned to face him.

"Well?" she demanded belligerently. "I trust you know your behavior borders on the offensive?"

"And yours borders on the shrewish," he returned in kind, leaning one broad shoulder against a pillar and studying her with a maddening smile. "Or have you some explanation for that childish display you treated us to before dinner?"

Pip's cheeks flamed at the words. "I am sure I do not know what you mean, your lordship," she muttered, presenting him her back as she turned to stare out into the shadows of the garden.

"Oh, I think you do." Alex pushed himself away

from the pillar and strode over to stand beside her. "You were deliberately baiting Miss Kingsford, and well you know it."

The injustice of that remark brought Pip spinning around. "And I suppose I was expected to sit there and meekly endure her slights and jabs!" she charged furiously, her chin coming up.

"As a matter of fact, you were." Alex's eyes gleamed in the moonlight as he stared down at her stormy expression. "Or you might have come to me for protection. I am more than capable of dealing with vicious females of Miss Kingsford's caliber."

"Doubtlessly that is because you have more experience of them!" Pip shot back, incensed by the very suggestion that she should turn to Alex—to any man—for assistance.

"Perhaps I have," Alex snapped, furious that she could so blithely court scandal with little thought for the consequences. "But that is beside the point. You should have ignored Miss Kingsford's remarks. A lady would have—"

"A lady was not the one being insulted." Pip was stung by yet another reminder how ineligible she must seem to him. "*I* was! And I am not about to allow anyone to make sport of me—something you would do well to remember, your lordship!"

"What the devil do you mean by that?" Alex demanded, grasping her roughly by the shoulders and drawing her against him. He remembered Kingsford's comments about her cleverness and wondered if somehow she had learned the truth.

The truth burned on Pip's tongue, but she found herself unable to utter it. "Nothing," she said at last, pushing ineffectually against his broad shoulders. "Now release me at once, or I vow I will box your ears until you howl!"

Alex glared down into her angry face. The moonlight gave her skin a pearly gleam, and turned her eyes into sparkling pools of forest green. His anger gave way to the passion he had so long repressed, and unable to help himself he lowered his head and took her mouth in a searing kiss.

The first touch of his lips on hers shocked Pip into immobility. It wasn't the first time she had been kissed, but it was the first time she found herself wanting to kiss in return. Alex felt so good, his body burning hard and warm against hers, that her mouth softened beneath his. Her eyes drifted shut as she abandoned herself to the wonderful sensations assaulting her senses, accepting at last the part of her she had always denied.

"Phillipa." Alex groaned in desire, delighting in her response. "Say now you will accompany me to the prince's. You are so beautiful, I cannot wait to show you off."

It took a moment for the words to penetrate Pip's conscience, but when they did it was with devastating effect. She drew back, passion turning to the pain of betrayal. Her eyes met his in disbelief, and then she was fighting her way out of his arms. The moment she was free, her hand lashed across his cheek in a stinging blow.

Alex stared down at her, silently cursing the momentary madness that had led to his making the offer. He raised a hand and touched the red mark left by her hand. "Your next words, I believe, are 'How dare you, sir,' " he said, fighting vainly for control. He couldn't believe he had bungled things so badly, and wondered if he would ever be able to set them right.

Pip, who had just been about to say those very words, drew herself up in haughty fury. "I know full well how you dare, your lordship," she said in icy contempt. "Because you are an unconscionable cad who would do whatever it takes to win his way! Well, you may save your lovemaking for some other fool. I would not go to Carlton House with you were you the last man in England!" And with that she turned and fled from the balcony, her yellow skirts trailing after her.

Alex watched her go with a heavy heart, bitterly telling himself he deserved little better. His only hope now of ever seeing her again was the ride home tomorrow. Perhaps once she had calmed down he would be able to convince her of his sincerity. If not . . . he cursed furiously, his expression tortured as he whirled around and stormed back into the drawing room. He was so lost in thought that he never saw the two men standing in the shadows, following his progress with undisguised interest.

Eight

Pip stormed back into her rooms in a black fury. Of all the low, vile, deceitful tricks, she fumed, flinging her fan on to the dressing table. Alex was a beast, a villain, a . . . She knew the perfect word to describe him, but she was far too much of a lady to utter it, even in her mind. But she would make him pay, she vowed, blinking back scalding tears. Somewhere, somehow she would make him pay.

After dismissing the maid, she donned her night rail and went to bed, but she was far too agitated to sleep. She lay abed for what seemed forever until she finally admitted defeat and got up. She'd just lit the taper by her bed when she heard a tentative knock on her door. Now what? she wondered crossly, stalking across the floor to tear open the door. The sight of Lydia hovering on her threshold brought her up short.

"Thank heaven you are still awake," Lydia exclaimed, crowding into the room before Pip had time to object. "I must speak with you."

Pip fell back obligingly, noting with some surprise that Lydia was still in her evening gown and diamonds. She'd heard the other guests retiring hours ago and assumed her hostess had followed suit. She hoped the other woman hadn't come to renew their squabble, for she was in no mood to pull caps with her.

"I–I see you are already dressed for bed," Lydia

stammered, a nervous smile coming and going on her lips.

Pip glanced down at her lawn night robe. "Yes, I have," she agreed, wondering what on earth was wrong with Lydia. "Is there something wrong? My aunt?" Her voice rose slightly as the possibility suddenly occurred to her.

"Oh—oh no, nothing like that," Lydia assured her with a hasty smile. "It is just . . . well . . . it is the most embarrassing thing, really, but it is about your room."

"My room?" Pip echoed, a suspicion forming in her mind.

"Yes." Lydia's voice regained some of its confidence. "My grandmother, Lady Elizabeth Harwicke, has only just arrived, and she is demanding to be shown to her usual room—this room," she added delicately, lest Pip fail to take the hint.

Pip's brow cleared as her suspicions were confirmed. So that was the way of it, she thought knowingly. She'd displeased her waspish hostess, and now the other woman was retaliating by evicting her from the elegant room.

"I realize what a terrible imposition this is," Lydia rattled on, "but the old dear is quite adamant. She often stays with us, and this is quite her favorite room in the house. I do hate to ask—"

"Say no more, Lydia," Pip interrupted, holding up her hand. "I understand perfectly. Naturally it would not do to inconvenience her ladyship."

Lydia's nervousness vanished as if it had never been. "Dearest Phillipa! I knew I could count upon you!" she gushed, laying her hand on Pip's arm. "Thank you for being so understanding."

"Not at all," Pip murmured, hiding her amusement. "Where would you like me to go?"

"I thought to put you with your aunt. Such an inconvenience, I know, but with all the other guests I'm afraid there aren't any available rooms. You don't mind, do you?"

"Certainly not. In fact I—"

"There, I knew you wouldn't object." Lydia was fairly beaming. "You are the *kindest* person!"

Pip's eyebrows rose at Lydia's effusive praise. Lady Harwicke must be rich indeed if Lydia was this eager to please her, she thought with a cynical smile. Oh well— she gave a mental shrug—it didn't matter a tick to her where she slept. It was only for one night, after all.

"I am happy to oblige," she said with a regal smile, inclining her head. "Now if you will send up a maid to help me pack, I shall be on my way."

"Oh, there is no need for that!" Lydia exclaimed with a horrified look. "That is, they can see to it while they are unpacking Grandmother's things."

This sounded rather confusing to Pip, although she supposed it might expedite matters. "Very well," she said reluctantly, "I will just change into—"

"Oh no, it will be better if you are in your night-clothes!"

"Better?" Pip looked puzzled.

"Faster," Lydia corrected, grasping Pip's arm again. "It will be much faster if you just go as you are. I mean, you'll just have to change once you get there, won't you?"

Pip considered that for a moment. "I suppose. But what if I should encounter one of the other guests? It is hardly proper to be running about in my night things."

"They are all in bed," Lydia assured her, pulling her toward the door. "Now if you don't mind, we really must hurry. Poor Grandmother is almost asleep on her feet. It is right this way."

Pip allowed Lydia to drag her out of the room and down the long shadow-filled hallway. She recalled Lydia's mentioning that Mrs. Beachton had been placed in the east wing, but it seemed to her they were headed west. She was about to mention this when she thought better of it. Surely Lydia must know the lay of her own house, she reasoned, and given her own admittedly poor sense of direction it was more than possible she was mistaken. Still she was careful to note their path so that she could retrace her steps if necessary without getting lost.

Her fears were put to rest several minutes later when Lydia halted outside of a brass-studded door. "This is your aunt's room," she whispered, holding a silencing finger up to her lips. "I had the chambermaid lay out some blankets and bedclothes on the settee, as she told me your aunt was already asleep."

"Oh, there's no need to whisper," Pip answered, although she was careful to keep her voice low-pitched. "My aunt is slightly hard of hearing, and when she sleeps, she is like one of the dead. You needn't fear I shall disturb her."

"That is good to know." Lydia's smile didn't quite reach her eyes. "We wouldn't want to awaken her. Now, if you'll excuse me, I must get down to my grandmother. She'll be wanting to retire." And she scurried away before Pip could stop her.

Pip gave her retreating figure a puzzled look. Really, there was no understanding the creature, she thought, opening the heavy door and stepping inside.

She'd half expected to find a small, insignificant room, and was agreeably surprised by the opulence of the Tudor-styled bedchamber. The furnishings were heavy and richly carved, especially the massive four-poster bed with its gold velvet curtains. A fireplace, its stones darkened by the smoke of generations of fires, dominated the far wall, and set in front of it was a brocade-covered settee piled high with blankets and feather pillows. She walked over to the settee, noting its small size with vague dismay.

It didn't look at all comfortable, she decided, her eyes flicking to the drawn curtains of the bed. Perhaps she would just slip into bed with her aunt and . . . A sonorous rumble emanating from behind the curtains halted her thought, and she turned back to the settee with a sigh. Oh well, she thought philosophically, picking up a blanket and carefully unfolding it, the settee might not be the most comfortable bed in the house, but it would have to do. And as she had already observed, it was only for one night. She could endure it.

He couldn't say what woke him. One minute he was sleeping peacefully, and the next he was wide awake, his battle-honed senses screaming a warning. He lay perfectly still for several seconds, straining to catch any sound, but when he heard nothing he opened the curtains and peeked cautiously about the room. Save for the fire burning low and red in the grate, the room was in darkness, and it took awhile for his eyes to adjust.

He rose cautiously, pulling on his dressing gown as he walked slowly about the room. He had just convinced himself he must have been dreaming when a soft sigh sounded behind him. He whirled around, his eyes widening at the sight of the figure huddled on the settee. What the hell . . . ? Then one of the blankets shifted, revealing the face he knew as well as his own.

He crossed the room in three strides, his control exploding with raw fury. Thinking only of betrayal, he reached down and grabbed Phillipa by the shoulders, administering a none-too-gentle shake as he pulled her to her feet.

"Damn you, Phillipa!" he roared, giving her another shake. "How could you do this to me?"

Her eyes finally fluttered open, and when they did he read the confusion in their emerald depths. "Alex?" She blinked up at him in what he could swear was confusion. "What are you doing in my aunt's room?"

He stared down at her, momentarily nonplussed by her sleepy demand, then his temper flared back to life. "Don't give me that, you scheming bitch," he accused, pain and anger combining in a potent mixture of emotion. "Just tell me what the devil you mean to gain by this trick, because I'll be damned if I'll marry you!"

"Marry you?" Phillipa gaped up at him, still trying to make sense of what was happening. She had been sleeping, dreaming she was eighteen again and standing in resentful silence as her father rang a peal over her head. He was scolding her for something—selling his best pipe, if memory served—and in the very next second he had become Alex, accusing her of some vile crime. Now Alex was standing before her, his hands heavy on her shoulders as he hurled hate-filled words at her. It had to be a dream, she decided desperately, because if it was reality then she had surely lost her mind.

"That's right, marriage," Alex continued with a bitter laugh, scarce believing Phillipa could have done this to him. "You must know we are compromised now. You have spent the night in my room."

"No!" Phillipa was becoming horribly aware that she was not dreaming. "This is my aunt's room! Lydia brought me here herself!"

"Don't lie, Phillipa." Alex released her and swung around, unable to look into her lying, innocent eyes for another moment. He couldn't remember ever being this furious in his life—or this hurt. It was as if his heart had been ripped out, leaving only a huge, gaping hole that was filling with pain.

That accusation was all it took to break the paralysis holding Pip in its coils. "Don't you dare call me a liar, you–you liar!" she railed, her temper rising to meet his. "You're the one who burst into my aunt's bedchamber without so much as knocking, and you can be very sure that—"

"Your *aunt's* bedchamber?" He gave a harsh laugh but did not turn around. "This is *my* bedchamber, my dear; *mine*. And it has been since the moment we arrived."

The blood drained from Phillipa's face. "But–but Lydia—"

"Don't try laying this on Miss Kingsford's doorstep." Alex turned around, his face so harsh and cold it might have been carved from stone. "This is all your doing! Why don't you just own up to the truth and be done with it? It's obvious you meant to trap me so that I would be forced to marry you."

Pip drew herself up proudly at his sneering words. "Don't flatter yourself, sir," she said coldly, hiding her anger and hurt behind an uncaring facade. "As if I would want such an arrogant and useless rake."

"Rake! Why you—"

"And furthermore," Pip continued as if he hadn't spoken, "it was never our intention that you should marry me. You're supposed to marry Belle."

"What?"

Pip clapped a hand over her mouth, her eyes widening in horror as she realized what she had said.

"What do you *mean* I am supposed to marry Miss Portham?" Alex demanded in bewilderment. He recalled the time one of his father's hunters had kicked him in the head; he'd been unconscious for almost ten minutes, and his head had rang for hours afterwards. He felt just like that now, and for one wild moment he wondered if he'd gone mad without realizing it.

Pip's temper had vanished the moment the angry words had left her mouth. Much as she would like to recant them, she knew that was impossible. She had no choice now but to tell all. Setting her chin at a defiant angle, she proceeded to do just that, relating in clipped, precise phrases the details of the scheme she and Belle had devised.

Alex listened in absolute silence, his emotions swinging from horrified disbelief to cold fury. "Do you mean to say," he began, his voice rigid with control, "that you and Miss Portham planned to marry me off as if I was a brainless dolt?"

Pip bristled in indignation. "Certainly not!" she denied hotly. "We never once called you a dolt."

"Well, thank God for that."

"I believe the term 'fashionable fribble' may have been used, but I assure it was not meant with disrespect."

"Fribble?" Alex's voice rose several octaves. *"Fribble?"*

"I told you, we meant no disrespect," Pip plowed on, with a mounting sense of self-righteousness. "It is just that in the very beginning we took you for something of a dilettante. We—"

"Dilettante?" Alex wondered how many more shocks he could take in one night. He had to have gone mad, he decided with a detached sense of calm. It was the only rational explanation.

"Of course. Given your poor attendance at Parliament and your rather dashing reputation with the muslin set, it seemed a logical conclusion to reach. But when my aunt informed us of your distinguished war record, we naturally reevaluated our opinion. And really, it all worked out for the better because Belle decided she preferred a man of honor after all."

Alex sat in stunned silence, trying to assimilate what he had just heard. There was one thing he understood all too well, and the very thought of it filled him with a deepening sense of outrage. "So the two of you decided that Miss Portham and I should make a match of it," he said slowly, taking deep, calming breaths. "It never once occurred to you that I might not wish to marry, or indeed, that I might have some other bride in mind?"

"Well, naturally if you were affianced to another we would have understood," Pip said, conveniently forgetting her own trepidation on the matter. "And as for your not wishing to marry—what man ever does? But you must marry sometime, if only to secure the succession, and Belle would make you the perfect viscountess. She is beautiful, wealthy—how can you possibly object?"

"Perhaps I object to being led like a stallion to the breeding pens," Alex said bluntly, his eyes dark with emotion. "Miss Portham may be as rich as Croesus, but that doesn't mean she can buy me."

"She wasn't trying to buy you!" Pip protested, although she supposed it probably sounded very much as if she were. "Besides, I scarce see where you have any right to stand in judgement of Belle and me. At least *we* weren't placing bets on the outcome!"

The bottom dropped out of Alex's stomach. "What?" he asked dully, praying he had misunderstood.

Pip felt a momentary smugness at his shattered expression. "You heard me. And I might say I was shocked to hear how you had schemed to use me. Wagering on whether or not I would accompany you to Carlton House is hardly the action of a gentleman!"

"You knew about the bet?"

"Of course. I heard it from Belle, who heard it from a friend, who heard it from her employer's husband." When he uttered a strangled oath, she gave him an impatient look. "Well, you certainly didn't think you could keep such a thing quiet, did you?"

Alex ran a weary hand over his face. "I tried," he muttered with a heavy sigh. "God knows I tried."

Pip believed him. Despite her annoyance, she knew he would never intentionally harm her, and her anger slowly subsided. As it faded, awareness of their tenuous situation crept in, and her eyes dropped from his.

"Yes, well, that is neither here nor there," she said, tightening the sash on her robe as she turned away. "At the moment, we have more pressing matters to consider."

"Your presence in my room," Alex agreed, relieved she was finally being sensible. "You say Miss Kingsford brought you here?"

"Yes," Pip said, and told him of Lydia's visit to her room. "I thought at the time she was displacing me because I had angered her," she concluded with a bitter

laugh. "But I had no idea I had angered her *this* much!
She certainly has had her revenge on me."

Alex managed a half-smile at her words. "If it's any
comfort, I don't think she arranged this to spite you.
More like she did it to help her brother." And he gave
her the details of Reginald's heavy wagering.

Pip was quick to see the implications. "The beast!
He was rigging the bet in his favor!" She shot Alex a
suspicious scowl. "Is that legal?"

"I don't know about legal, but it certainly isn't honorable," Alex told her, his lips thinning with fury. "Unfortunately, there is little I can do about it."

"Of course you can do something about it!" she
snapped, annoyed he should be such a slow top. "Don't
take me to the ball. You have only to do that and that
miserable snake will lose everything."

Alex gave her an incredulous look. "You can't be serious," he said at last. "You must know that the situation between us has changed. Whether or not it was any
of our doing, we have been compromised, and there is
nothing we can do but announce our engagement."

"Engagement?" Now it was Pip who wondered if she
had taken leave of her senses.

"Certainly." Alex drew himself up proudly. "I am a
gentleman. And although your actions often indicate the
opposite, you are a lady. Given the situation, what other
choice have we?"

Pip glared at him, caught between her anger and the
awful knowledge that he was right. Worst of all was the
realization that the more he insisted they must marry,
the more tempting the idea became. When she began
envisioning herself in a bridal gown, she knew she had
to do something.

"We must be logical," she said decisively, forcing her
mind to function. "If we look hard enough, I am sure
we can find some way out of this contretemps."

"Like what?"

"I don't know! Something." Her brows met as she

considered their situation from every conceivable angle. As he had been so good to point out, things did indeed look bleak. Not only were they in the same bedchamber together, but the house just happened to be filled with several of the worst gossips in England. If even one of them was to learn of this, then their reputations were both forfeit. Unless . . .

"Who knows this is your bedchamber?" she asked suddenly.

"Anyone who would take the trouble to enquire, I should suppose," Alex replied, his mind already on the difficulty of procuring a special license. He would have to send for the family's betrothal ring the moment he was back in London, he decided. And then there was the announcement to the newspapers to consider. It might be better if he sent it first. In that way, Phillipa would be under the protection of his name before the tongues could start wagging.

"Lydia brought me here," Pip continued, a daring plan unfolding in her mind. "No one saw us—I am sure of it—and she can't say anything without admitting her role in the matter. There is no way anyone will ever know."

That caught Alex's attention. "What the devil does that matter?" he demanded with a scowl. "*We* would know! Compromised is compromised."

"Oh, don't be such a prig." Pip moved toward the door, saying a silent prayer as she tested the door. To her relief, the handle turned easily, and she faced Alex with a triumphant smile. "Just as I thought; she didn't lock it. I'll just slip out and return to my own rooms before the rest of the house discovers us."

Alex shook his head in disbelief. "Weren't you listening to a word I said?" he demanded furiously. "Whether or not anyone can prove a bloody thing, the fact remains we have been compromised, and—"

"If you say that word one more time, I vow I shall

scream," Pip warned, hands on her hips as she returned his glare. "We have *not* been compromised."

"Then what would you call it?" Alex retorted, amazed that any woman could be so stubborn.

"Outmaneuvered."

"Damn it, Phillipa, this is not a game! Have you any idea what is at stake here?"

Pip's chin lifted at that. "What has been at stake since the moment you entered into this silly bet," she said with quiet dignity. "My reputation."

Her even reply brought a flush of shame to Alex's face. "I am aware of that," he said with as much grace as he could muster. "And believe me, I sincerely regret not having put an end to it when I had the chance. But none of that matters now. Bet or nay, my honor demands that I marry you."

His words thrust a sword into Pip's heart. "I have my honor, too," she told him, "and I cannot do as you say."

"Blast it, Phillipa—"

"You said you objected to being led like a . . . a stallion to the breeding pens," she interrupted, blushing at his frank analogy. "Well, so do I object to being led where I would not go. You speak of *your* honor, and what *you* must do—but what about me? Have I no say in this at all?"

It annoyed him that she could be so eloquent—and so right. Thrusting a hand through his hair, he gave her a defeated look. "I am only trying to do what is right," he said at last. "This is all my fault, and I will not have you suffer because of it."

Something deep inside of Pip relaxed. When, in spite of her protests, he had kept insisting they marry, he had put her uncomfortably in mind of her father, who had always ridden roughshod over her, ignoring her objections as if they had no validity. She might have known Alex was cut from a different cloth, she decided, moving forward to rest a hand on his arm.

"I realize that," she said, meeting his hooded gaze,

"and I appreciate it. But I still refuse to be forced into marriage because of a lot of idle prattle."

"What do you propose?" he asked, reluctantly accepting that at the moment there was little he could do to make her see the truth.

Her eyes went to the carved clock on the mantel. "It is barely four in the morning," she said, straining to read the gilded face. "Not even the servants should be about at this hour. I can still return to my rooms with no one the wiser."

"But what about Lady Harwicke?" Alex asked, raising whatever objections he could. "Didn't you say Miss Kingsford had given her your room?"

Pip shook her head at him. "You don't believe her, do you? It was obviously just a ruse to get me out of the way, and I blush to admit I fell for it. Had I stopped to consider the matter, I would have realized it was highly unlikely that an elderly lady would be arriving after midnight."

"And Reginald and Miss Kingsford? Do you really think they'll hold their tongues?" Alex pressed, with the tenacity that had seen him through so many years of war.

"Reginald I leave to you; I am sure you can convince him of the advisability of maintaining a prudent silence. As for Lydia, I shall deal with her in my own way. Now let us hear no more of the matter," Pip replied decisively, wishing he would be quiet. She was well aware of the dangers inherent in her scheme, and having him point out each and every one was doing little to soothe her lacerated nerves.

"But what if you encounter someone? What—"

"Alex!" Pip shot him an aggrieved look. "Do you *want* to marry me?"

"Of course not!" he answered quickly. "I am just trying to make you see reason."

"I do see reason; I just prefer to ignore it."

"Phillipa—"

"As to the other, we shall just have to hope my luck holds, won't we?" Pip concluded in a rush. "But might I point out that every second you delay me with your incessant protests, the greater that possibility becomes? At the rate you are going it will be daylight before I get out of here."

Alex's lips twitched. He knew the situation was far from laughable, yet he could not help himself. "Witch." He reached out to tug a curl that was straggling down from beneath her nightcap. "If I had an ounce of sense, I would let you go and say to the devil with the consequences. Unfortunately I am not sure that I can."

Pip tried not to flush at the feel of his warm fingers brushing her cheek. "If you mean to try and stop me . . ." she warned, taking a cautious step backwards.

"I am not so big a gudgeon as that," he assured her, an odd smile playing across his lips. "I know when to admit defeat."

"You do?" Pip wasn't sure if she was relieved or annoyed.

"Mmm." He touched her cheek again. "Just promise me one thing."

"What?"

Alex smiled at the suspicion in her voice. "If you should encounter anyone, I want you to come directly back to me. I will take care of it from there."

"How?" she wanted to know.

"Never mind. Just promise me."

Pip realized she had no other choice, and grudgingly gave her word. "Oh, very well, you wretch, but I shan't marry you, regardless of who I encounter."

He ignored that. "You'd better go," he said instead, crossing the room to open the door. "As you say, every second you're here increases your chance of discovery."

Pip bit back an impatient retort and followed him to the door. Men, she thought sourly, brushing past him to peek up and down the darkened hallway. They really were the most vexing creatures. With that thought up-permost in her mind, she slipped out into the hall, her heart in her throat as she made a mad dash for the safety of her room.

Nine

The sound of rattling dishes woke Pip several hours later, and she rolled over just as the young maid assigned her entered the room with her pot of morning chocolate. Lydia and another woman were hot on her heels, and had she harbored any doubts as to her hostess's involvement, those doubts would have been squashed by the look of almost comical dismay that flashed across her face.

"Why, good morning, Lydia," Pip said, hiding her fury behind a sleepy smile. "Whatever brings you and Miss Gervey here at this hour?"

"I . . . but you . . . how . . . ?" Lydia sputtered incoherently for several seconds before gaining control over herself. "I beg your pardon," she said stiffly, her hands clenched at her side, "but Miriam and I were about to set out on our morning ride, and we thought perhaps you would like to join us."

So *that's* how they plotted "accidentally" to find her in Alex's rooms, Pip thought furiously. When it was discovered her bed hadn't been slept in, a search would naturally have been conducted, and of course Alex would have to be notified. She could almost see it now: the feigned shock, the dignified embarrassment as she and Alex were found together. Lydia would undoubtedly have sworn her silence, as befits a hostess faced with two misbehaving guests, but Miriam Gervey would have been under no such obligation, and she was the biggest tattler in England. Thank God Alex had awoken in time.

"A morning ride sounds delightful," she assured Lydia, patting back a delicate yawn. "Only give me a few minutes to change, and I shall meet you ladies in the stable."

A bright stain of color washed over Lydia's cheeks, but her voice was even as she said, "Very well, we shall see you then." She swung around and stalked out, leaving poor Miriam no choice but to trail after her.

The ride was as short as it was uncomfortable, and the three ladies soon returned to the house for breakfast. Lydia looked fit to break something, while Miriam behaved like a sulky child denied a promised treat. Both of them were stiffly polite to Pip, a circumstance which only added to her determination to make Lydia pay for her treachery. She carefully bided her time, waiting until the other guests had filed down for the morning meal before springing her trap.

"By the by, Lydia," she said with every evidence of friendship, "I had the oddest dream about you last night."

Lydia gave a guilty start, the tea in her cup sloshing over its rim. "Indeed?" she said coldly. "How interesting."

"Oh, yes," Pip continued, aware the other guests were listening with varying degrees of interest. "I dreamed I had gone to bed and that you came to my room and asked me to move to another room, as you needed mine for another guest. Then you said you would take me to my aunt's rooms, but instead you took me to the wrong room. Isn't that funny?"

Lydia's hands shook as she attempted to butter her bread. "Hilarious," she agreed with a sick smile, obviously at a loss as to what she should do.

"What room did she take you to, Miss Lambert?"

one of the male guests obliged her by asking. "Not mine, I trust? Heh, heh."

"Mr. Yale!" Pip gave his hand a playful swat. "Shame on you! As a matter of fact, I am not quite sure where she took me, only that it seemed quite dark and mysterious. When the maid awoke me this morning, I was still confused, and I cannot tell you how relieved I was to find myself safely in my own bed. Have you ever had a dream like that, Lydia?" She pinned Lydia with a falsely sweet smile.

"No, I have not." Lydia drained her cup and turned to the footman. "Brandy," she ordered in a clipped tone, "and be quick about it."

If the other guests thought it odd their hostess should be imbibing at such an early hour, they were too well bred to say so, and the conversation turned to other matters. Alex didn't appear until about halfway through the rather strained meal, his left hand wrapped in a bandage. One of the other guests were quick to note it, and Alex dismissed his interest with a shrug.

"I closed a door on it," he said, his cool tone discouraging any further questions.

There was another silence as the other guest applied themselves diligently to their meals. Pip, however, was not to be dissuaded and began pestering Lydia again.

"Wherever is your dear brother?" she asked, glancing about with wide eyes. "I was sure he would be here to see his guests safely off. I do hope he isn't ill."

"I have no idea," Lydia said peevishly. "I am not his keeper!"

"Oh?" Pip's eyebrows arched in mock surprise. "And here I thought you were devoted to each other. As an only child, I quite longed for a brother or a sister. I used to imagine the scrapes we would fall into, and how we would help each other out of them. I am sure you would help Reginald if he found himself in difficulty, wouldn't you?"

Lydia tossed down her napkin, her face purpling with rage. "I have had about enough of—"

"What time will you and your aunt be ready, Miss Lambert?" Alex asked, deciding he too had had enough—of watching Phillipa torture Miss Kingsford. To be sure, the witch deserved it, but if Phillipa kept it up, she was certain to rouse suspicion.

"Whenever you would like, your lordship," Pip replied shortly, annoyed with him for spoiling her fun.

"Then I should like to leave at once," Alex informed her decisively. "I have business in London which requires my immediate attention. Shall we say ... two hours?"

The superior way he arched his eyebrows made Pip long to reject his request, but in the end she thought better of it. She'd already learned he was not to be pushed, and in any case she'd had more than enough of Thorn Hill and the Kingsfords. "Very well, sir," she said, inclining her head graciously. "I will go now and let Aunt know we shall be leaving."

She made her gracious goodbyes to the other guests before turning to Lydia. "Thank you so much for your kind hospitality," she said with a cloying smile. "I'm not sure I can ever repay you for all you've done, but I daresay I'll think of something. *Au revoir.*"

"You shouldn't have said that, Phillipa." Alex's voice was reproachful as the carriage made its way toward London. "You'd already routed her; there was no need to rub her face in it as well."

"Ha!" Pip gave an indignant sniff, her shoulders hunched as she huddled in her corner of the coach. "You are soldier enough to know victory must be absolute, especially when one is dealing with a vicious baggage like Lydia Kingsford! Believe me, she will know better than to spread a word about last night."

Alex could have told her as much. He'd already beaten a similar assurance out of Reginald, and he was

satisfied with the dandy's terrified promise to control
Lydia. Not that it mattered. As he'd told Phillipa, compromised was compromised.

"I know no good ever comes from humiliating one's
enemies," he said coolly, folding his arms across his
chest. "It only makes them that much more determined
to seek revenge."

"Well, she is welcome to try," Pip continued, ignoring her aunt, who was snoring peacefully beside her.
"She might think herself the cleverest cat in the house,
but she's yet to cross swords with Belle. When I tell her
about this stunt, she'll—"

Alex's arms dropped as he sat upright. "Do you
mean you're going to tell her about"—His eyes flicked
uneasily in Mrs. Beachton's direction—"about last
night?" he concluded with a hiss.

"I'd planned to, yes," Pip admitted, wincing at the
thought of how she'd failed her dearest friend. "This
was all her idea, and it is only right that she be informed. I only hope she won't be too disappointed. She
was so looking forward to a summer wedding."

"Your pardon, I am sure, for failing to oblige a lady,"
Alex muttered stiffly, piqued by her determination to
marry him off to another woman.

Pip drew herself up at the biting words. "There is no
need to be sarcastic, sir," she informed him.

"No need . . ." Alex's voice trailed off. "Upon my
soul, Phillipa! You and your monied friend scheme to
snatch me up as if I were a bauble in a shop window,
and then you tell me there is no need to be sarcastic?
What the blazes do you expect me to be? Grateful?"

"Will you kindly lower your voice?" Pip hissed,
shooting her snoring aunt a pointed look. "And no, I do
not expect you to be grateful. Although I do think you
might be flattered. Belle is considered a prime catch,
you know."

"I believe you mentioned it last night," Alex answered, his eyes narrowing as he studied her face. He

wondered if she was still intent on fostering this absurd match between her friend and himself, despite all that had happened. If so, he felt it only fair that he should disabuse her of that notion as soon as possible. He leaned back against the squabs, assuming a deliberately indolent pose.

"Speaking of Miss Portham, you must know there is no way I can marry her now, even if I wanted to," he said, his voice cool.

Pip became fascinated with the strings of her reticule. "I do not see why," she mumbled, not meeting his piercing gaze. "To be sure, our actions might be considered a trifle unconventional, but that doesn't mean you should reject the marriage out of hand. Belle would make you a—"

"Perfect viscountess," he finished for her. "I know, but that changes nothing. To quote Caesar, 'the die is cast.' "

Pip thought he was talking of his pride, and grew impatient. "You are being monstrously unfair!" she charged, wrapping the strings of her reticule tighter about her fingers. "Is what Belle and I did any different from what any matchmaking mama might have done? They call it 'the marriage mart,' for heaven's sake! We were just being honest in our goals."

Alex would have liked to refute her argument, but as his own actions were so lacking in honor, he did not feel he had that right. And, in a way, she was telling the truth. Society did exist for the sole purpose of arranging marriages, although it galled him to admit as much. Still . . .

"Do you want me to marry Miss Portham?" he asked, studying her face. "You seem rather intent upon the match."

The blunt question made Pip face an issue she had been avoiding since she and Alex set out for Thorn Hill. *Did* she want him to marry Belle, she asked herself, and was shaken by the immediate but definite answer. "It is not so much that I 'want' you to marry," she said, choosing her words with almost painful care. "It is just that I . . . I feel Belle is right, and that for a female in her circumstances, marriage is the best possible answer."

"What about a female in your circumstances?" Alex asked curiously. "Wouldn't marriage serve you just as well?"

Pip's head came snapping up. "Oh, no!" she said quickly, her green eyes earnest. "I shall *never* marry."

The certainty in her voice set Alex back apace. "Never?" he echoed.

Pip nodded. "Marriage is the prison house designed by men to enslave women," she said, repeating the words that until quite recently she had believed with all her heart, "and I do not intend to willingly incarcerate myself."

Alex could only stare at her, shocked into silence. Such an adamant stand did not bode well for the future, he realized with an uneasy swallow. "But what about children?" he asked, praying she was only twitting him. "Surely you want them? All women want children."

A sudden image of a mischievous dark-haired imp sent a sharp pain piercing through Pip's heart. "Naturally, I should like a child," she said with as much dignity as she could muster, "but there is little I can do about it. I might admire Wollstonecraft's political philosophy, but that doesn't mean I intend to emulate her in every way."

The news that she wanted children came as a profound relief, and Alex released the breath he had been holding. "I did not mean to imply you would," he said evenly. "I was but pointing out that good can come out of anything . . . even the evil 'prison' of marriage."

She had to smile at his playful tone. "So you are now an advocate of matrimony, your lordship?" she asked, peeking up at him through her thick lashes. "Your friends would be astounded."

"My friends might understand better than you think," he said, thinking of Marcus. "You ladies are not the only ones who sometimes have no other recourse."

A loud snort and grumble from Mrs. Beachton spared Pip the necessity of answering his rather oblique comment. "Oh, my," the elderly lady exclaimed, straightening her clothing with obvious embarrassment. "I did not mean to nod off like that. Have I been sleeping long?"

"A few miles only," Alex soothed, silently cursing her poor timing. He'd hoped to secure Phillipa's agreement to their marriage before reaching London. Now he would have to proceed without it.

Perhaps it was all for the best, he decided, turning his gaze out the window as Phillipa and her aunt began discussing the scenery. Given her amazing attitude toward marriage it might be wisest to present her with a *fait accompli*. For all her radical nonsense, she wasn't wholly lost to reason. Once their engagement was announced, she'd fall into line soon enough. At least, he amended ruefully, he hoped she would.

The two days following her return to London were filled with frustration for Pip. Not only had Belle chosen the first part of the week to return to her house in the Cotswolds, but Alex was also missing. She'd overheard one of her aunt's gossiping friends say he'd left for his estates the very day of their return, and surmised this meant he'd settled his accounts at his club and had left town until the dust settled. While she understood his reasons for doing so, she couldn't help but feel piqued he hadn't contacted her before leaving. So much for his fine talk about protecting her, she decided with a sniff.

On the third day of her return, she was setting out for the lending library when Belle came bursting into the room, a newspaper clutched in her hand. "Have you seen this?" she demanded, thrusting the newspaper under Pip's nose.

Pip glanced down at the newsprint. "Not another fete for Wellington?" she asked, dutifully reading the article Belle indicated. "The poor man must be feeling feted to death with—"

"No, not that article," Belle interrupted, jabbing the paper with her finger. "This!"

Pip glanced at the column marked next to the article. "Marriages Announced. Really, Belle, what makes you think I give a fig about . . ." Her voice trailed off, her eyes widening in stunned disbelief at the primly worded announcement.

His lordship, Alexander George Wainwright Daltry, Viscount St. Ives, announces his engagement to Miss Phillipa Augusta Lambert, spinster. A wedding at the viscount's country estate is expected.

The newspaper shook in her hands as she reread the announcement. "This is a mistake," she mumbled, as if saying the words would somehow make it so. "This *has* to be a mistake."

Belle gave her a startled look. "Then you knew nothing of this? You're not engaged to St. Ives?"

"No," Pip denied with a vigorous shake of her head. "How could you believe such a thing of me?"

"Well, what else was I to believe when I looked down and saw that?" Belle defended herself pragmatically. "I was drinking a cup of tea at the time, and when I began choking Miss Cates pounded me on the back so vigorously I almost ended up in my porridge."

"Miss Cates?" The name was not familiar to Pip.

"My newest companion, and a most accomplished lady," Belle explained, smiling at the thought of her newest *protégée*. Belle had had a succession of companions, gently-bred ladies fallen on hard times whom she trained for, and helped find, positions that would provide them with financial security. "You will like her, Pip, for she is a most accomplished lady. Her father was a don at Oxford, and she speaks four languages. I hope to have her placed in a situation within a month or two, although I fear it will not be an easy task. Miranda is not blessed with what one might call a biddable disposition."

In the next moment she was shaking her head. "You are trying to distract me!" she accused crossly. "We're supposed to be discussing your engagement to St. Ives."

"But that is just it, I am *not* engaged to Alex—to St. Ives," Pip amended. "And I have no idea how that wretched announcement got into the papers. Although—"

"Although what?"

Pip sighed, knowing she had put off telling Belle the truth for as long as she dared. "Although something *did* happen last weekend which might have something to do with this," she said. She proceeded to tell Belle of Saturday night's fiasco, having carefully rehearsed every word. By the time she was finished, Belle was in a rage.

"That witch!" she cried, her eyes flashing with anger as she paced up and down the room. "That—that infamous she-devil! Oh! By the time I am finished with that viper and her loose screw of a brother, they will be wishing themselves at Jericho! I—" she broke off suddenly. "You say St. Ives asked you to marry him?"

"Not asked, commanded," Pip corrected, amused by Belle's passionate defense of her. "And in a most odious tone of voice as well. He made it quite obvious he was only marrying me out of a sense of *noblesse oblige,* and that there was naught I could do but accept. Needless to say I rejected his heartfelt offer."

"And you're certain his lordship didn't send this announcement to the papers?" Belle began, tapping her foot. "It sounds precisely the high-handed sort of thing he would do."

"So it does," Pip agreed with a smile, "but I am positive he had naught to do with this. I made my refusal quite obvious, and he seemed to accept it like a gentleman. Besides, why should he bother? I told you no one suspects a thing."

"Perhaps because it's as he said, 'Compromised is compromised,' " Belle suggested, looking troubled. "You've mentioned more than once that he is a man who takes his obligations quite seriously."

"But there is no reason for him to think that," Pip persisted, her cheeks flushing as she remembered that intimate kiss in the garden. "Nothing happened!"

Belle noted the betraying blush, but was wise enough to hold her tongue. "Very well," she said, turning her agile mind to another matter. "But if neither you nor St. Ives is responsible for that announcement, then who is?"

"I have no idea," Pip answered truthfully. "I shouldn't put it past either Reginald or Lydia, or even that dolt Tobias Flanders. He was the one who first suggested the wager, you know."

"Mmm," Belle conceded, although she didn't sound convinced. "The culprit might also be any of the men who participated in the wager, which would make half the men in London suspect. Still, I do not suppose that it signifies one way or another."

"What do you mean by that?" Pip demanded with an aggrieved scowl. "Of course it signifies!"

"Not really." Belle was serious as she studied Pip. "You must know that this places both you and Lord St. Ives in an untenable position."

Pip was getting heartily sick of that particular sentiment. "It's not as bad as all that," she argued, a hint of desperation in her voice. "We can always demand the paper print a retraction, or we have simply to deny there *is* an engagement. Surely if we can prove we are the innocent victims of a cruel prank, society will understand."

"Perhaps."

"And even if it does not, what would it matter? We

can't be forced to marry ... can we?" She turned to Belle for reassurance.

Belle sighed. Worldly as Pip liked to think herself, she was still an innocent, especially in the ways of the *ton*. Much as Belle would have liked to pretend everything would be fine, she knew things were very bleak indeed.

"I think 'force' is rather too strong a word," she said, giving Pip a comforting smile. "But there is no denying that they can make things decidedly uncomfortable for both you and Lord St. Ives. Are you quite certain marriage is out of the question?"

Pip was horrified to find she was on the verge of tears. She hadn't felt this helpless since she was a small child, and the feeling left her bereft of hope. It was like being trapped in a bog, she thought, struggling for control. The harder she fought to free herself, the deeper she sank. "You know how I feel about marriage," she began, her voice shaking despite all her efforts.

"Indeed I do," Belle agreed gently, but with complete candor. "But this time it won't be the shroud you'll be choosing over the veil, it will be the mantle of disgrace. Do you really want that for either St. Ives or yourself?"

"Alex?" Pip gave a watery sniff.

Belle's patience snapped. "Oh, for heaven's sake, Pip! You don't think he can compromise you and then walk away unscathed? At the very least, he'd be branded an unprincipled rake, and at the worst, he would be called a seducer. Either way, it is unlikely he would be accepted into society for a very long time to come."

Pip paled into horror. She realized that until this very moment she'd been so wrapped up in worry over her own predicament that she hadn't given a thought to how Alex might be affected. "I ... but surely he would be forgiven," she protested, wincing at the thought of a man as proud as Alex subjected to such censure. "He is a man, after all, and a certain degree of rakishness is expected, if not encouraged. Indeed, he already has such a reputation!"

"There is a world of difference between taking a mistress from the muslin company and compromising a young lady of quality," Belle informed her bluntly. "The one, as you say, is expected, but the other would place St. Ives beyond the pale, and I cannot think you would really wish that upon him."

"But—"

There was a knock, and the butler entered with a low bow. "I beg your pardon, Miss Lambert," he said formally, "but Lord St. Ives has called for you. I have taken the liberty of putting him in the Blue Room, if that meets with your approval."

Pip turned to Belle, her green eyes filled with panic. "Oh, my heavens, he must have seen the announcement!" she cried, her face paling. "He'll think I placed it, and he'll be furious! You mustn't leave me, Belle, regardless of what he says!"

"Of course," Belle agreed soothingly. She turned to the butler, who was listening to their exchange with unabashed curiosity.

"You may inform his lordship that Miss Lambert and I shall be with him in a moment," she instructed in a crisp tone that had the butler snapping to attention.

"Very good, Miss Portham," he replied hastily, executing another deep bow. "And on behalf of myself and the staff, Miss Lambert, allow me to offer you our felicitations. This is a happy day for us all."

Pip managed a strangled "Thank you," but the moment the door closed behind him, she buried her face in her hands. "Oh, Lord, the staff knows!" she wailed. "If Aunt knows as well, then I am as good as married! She has been throwing Alex at my head since the moment we met. What am I going to do?"

"The first thing you are going to do is pull yourself together. And then you are going upstairs and change your clothes," Belle ordered, rising purposefully to her feet. "I will entertain his lordship until you arrive."

"But what about the announcement?" Pip was human enough to welcome the notion of a reprieve, however brief. "He is bound to be in a rage."

Belle drew herself up. "Do you think that would bother me?" she asked imperiously.

"No," Pip admitted, smiling at the thought of Alex and Belle facing each other across the drawing room. She would give a great deal to see who would emerge the victor.

"Good." Belle gave her a gentle push toward the door. "Now hurry. You wouldn't want St. Ives to think you have been crying over him, would you?"

Pip dashed a guilty hand across her eyes, annoyed with herself for dissolving into a watering pot. "I most certainly would not," she said with a return of her usual spirit.

"The thing to remember is that you are the innocent in all of this," Belle lectured, holding the door open for her. "You have done nothing of which to be ashamed. And besides, as you said, what can St. Ives do? He can't coerce you into marrying him, can he?"

Belle was right, Pip thought happily. When it came right down to it, there was very little Alex could do. The realization made her giddy with relief. "Very well," she said brightly, starting toward the door, "kindly tell Alex I will be with him in a few minutes. And Belle?"

"Yes?" Belle sounded somewhat harried.

"Thank you for everything," Pip said, pausing to give her a fond smile. "You've been a very good friend to me, and I thank you for it."

To her surprise, Belle looked as if she were about to burst into tears herself. "Thank you, Pip," she said in a strained voice. "I pray you will always feel that way."

Pip wanted to ask her what she meant, but then she

remembered that declarations of friendship only made Belle uncomfortable. She gave her a wordless hug and dashed upstairs to make herself presentable for the coming confrontation.

Ten

In the drawing room Alex was waging his own battle for control. He'd returned home from his estates late last night, the family's betrothal ring securely tucked in his pocket, and after a restless sleep he'd awakened feeling bleary-eyed and edgy. He had been enjoying a leisurely breakfast when the sight of the announcement—posted a full two days ahead of schedule—sent him into a black fury. His first reaction was to storm down to Fleet Street and demand the clerk's head, but now that he'd had time to consider the matter he decided that perhaps it was all for the best. Now that the engagement had been announced, Phillipa would have to marry him.

The thought of Phillipa as his wife filled him with an odd mixture of emotions. The few times he'd given marriage any thought at all, he'd pictured himself marrying some wellborn miss who would give him an heir and then leave him alone—in other words, a society marriage. Certainly he'd never imagined he'd be placed in the awkward position of marrying a troublesome bluestocking as the only way of avoiding a scandal. Yet strangely enough, he felt no resentment. A man could do worse, he decided with a half-smile. And with Phillipa as his wife, at least he wouldn't have to worry about ever being bored.

The door opened behind him, and he turned to find

Miss Portham regarding him with a look of imperious disdain. "Miss Lambert will be joining us in a moment, your lordship," she told him in frosty accents. "Will you not be seated?"

Alex reluctantly took his seat, feeling like a shabby schoolboy who had fallen into his governess's bad graces. He recalled what Phillipa had said about Belle's making a wonderful viscountess, and sent a silent prayer heavenward that he would be spared the agony of proposing to her. It would take a braver man than he to storm that icy citadel, he mused with singular relief.

As if privy to his thoughts, Belle gave him a cool smile. "Pip tells me she has informed you of my hopes for an alliance," she said, with all the indifference of one discussing the weather. "I am sorry you have decided we would not suit."

Alex's face turned a dull red. "I meant no insult to you, ma'am, I assure you," he said, wishing the chair would simply open up and swallow him. "It is just a man prefers to do his own courting. Although I do thank you for the ... er ... honor."

Belle inclined her head regally, hiding a small smile at his discomfiture. "Thank you for the information, your lordship. I shall remember to keep that in mind for future reference."

Alex wondered what she meant by that, then decided he was better off not knowing. He did, however, think it wise to let her know that whatever her plans, they had best not include his wife.

"You and Phillipa have known each other quite long, have you not?" he asked, striving for the brisk tone he had used to command his troops.

"Seven years, your lordship," Belle answered, her eyebrows arching both at his tone and at his casual use of Pip's given name.

"Good. Then I shall look forward to your visiting us at St. Ives after we are married," he finished, with far more confidence than he felt. "I am sure Phillipa will welcome your company."

A lifetime of hiding her deepest emotions was all that kept Belle from tumbling out of her chair in shock. "After you are married," she repeated, enunciating each word with the greatest care. "Am I to take it, then, that you have already proposed to Pip?"

"Certainly." Alex looked down the length of his nose at her. "What sort of gudgeon do you take me for?"

"And been accepted?" she pressed, thinking of Pip's shock when she'd seen the announcement.

Alex bit back an oath, disliking being forced into making explanations. "Naturally, Miss Lambert had some reservations," he began stiffly, "but now that she has had time to consider the matter I am sure she will see that there is really no other course of action. I take it she told you of this weekend?"

Belle nodded, and he continued, "Then you must agree that marriage is our only option. Despite what either of you may think of me, I have no intention of allowing her to be ruined."

"I am glad to hear that," Belle replied, admiring the viscount's integrity. "Otherwise I shouldn't have the slightest compunction about ruining *you*. And I could do it, your lordship, make no doubt of that."

Alex's blue eyes met her steady, golden gaze, and a smile spread across his face. "Oh, I believe you, Miss Portham," he said, his dislike slowly dissolving. "And may I say it pleases me to know that she has such a loyal friend in you?"

Belle was considering a suitable reply when Pip made her belated entrance. Determined to set the tone for the coming confrontation, she'd donned one of her most unbecoming gowns of brown bombazine, and her hair was pulled back in a tight bun. Alex rose to his feet to greet her, but before he could even open his mouth she launched into her hastily-prepared speech.

"I want you to know that neither Belle nor I had anything to do with that ridiculous announcement," she said, her green eyes shining with a martial light. "We believe it was Lydia or Reginald's doing, and I promise you we shall be contacting the papers."

"Phillipa." Alex shot Miss Portham an uneasy look. "I think this is something we ought to discuss when we are alone."

"Nonsense," Pip continued, wanting nothing more than to put an end to the uncomfortable farce. "There is no need for secrecy with Belle, for I have told her everything. Now, as I was about to say, we shall contact the papers at once. This is all an infamous lie, and if they don't print an immediate retraction, we shall threaten them with legal action. Belle has several solicitors, and I am sure she would be more than happy to recommend one to us."

"I have my own lawyers," Alex snapped, making a concentrated effort to seize control of the conversation. "And as for the Kingsfords—"

"Oh, you needn't think I've forgotten them!" Pip exclaimed, finding it easier to attack than to defend. "We shall force them to admit their treachery before the *ton*, and that should put an end to their scheming. There will still be some tattle because of the wager, but if we stand firm and deny everything, there is nothing anyone can do."

"I have no intention of denying anything, and furthermore, there is something I feel you should know—"

"And, of course, when I don't appear with you at the prince's ball, society will see this was all a humbug, and it will be dismissed as a nine days' wonder. I—"

"Damn it, Pip!" Alex was on his feet and glowering at her. "The Kingsfords didn't send that announcement to the papers. *I* did!"

Pip's jaw dropped. "You *what?*"

Alex turned to Belle. "Miss Portham," he said formally, "if you will excuse us, I would like to speak privately with my fiancée."

Pip had recovered from her shock and turned on Alex with flushed cheeks. "Belle is staying!" she insisted heatedly. "Nor am I your fiancée!"

"Forgive me, Pip, but I believe I shall do as St. Ives asks," Belle interrupted, rising to her feet. "I will call upon you tomorrow."

"But Belle—" Pip was dismayed to find herself near tears at the prospect of being deserted. "You promised!"

Belle shook her head. "No, Phillipa, his lordship is right. This is something best settled between the two of you—and alone."

"But—"

"Now, don't look so downcast," Belle interrupted, crossing the room to give her a quick hug. "It will all work out for the best, you'll see." She then turned to Alex who was regarding them with a watchful expression.

"Good day to you, your lordship," she said with a cool nod. "I trust you will remember what I have said?"

"I will, Miss Portham," he promised. "As I trust you will remember what I have said. I meant it, you know, every word."

Belle's mouth softened into a smile that revealed the full quota of her stunning beauty. "Yes," she said, secretly pleased. "I can see that you do. Goodbye." And she slipped quietly from the room, leaving Alex and Pip alone.

After an uncomfortable silence, Pip tossed her head back in a defiant gesture. "Well?" she demanded crossly. "Are you going to explain what that was about?"

"Just a private matter between Miss Portham and myself," Alex answered, wisely hiding his amusement from her too-knowing eyes. "Unlike you, she is capable on occasion of rational thought."

Pip gave a loud sniff, feeling piqued. "Then perhaps you ought to offer for her," she sniped. " 'Tis not too late, you know."

"Isn't it?" He gave her a mysterious smile that sent her heart rocking. "In the meanwhile, there is a small misunderstanding I would like to rectify. You *are* my fiancée, Phillipa, and as soon as it can be arranged, you will be my wife."

The calm certainty in his voice filled Pip with frustration. "But why?" she cried, not for the first time. "I keep telling you—there is no need!"

"And I keep telling you that there is," Alex returned, folding his arms across his chest and giving her a significant look. "Perhaps you are foolish enough to believe we can keep this quiet, but I do not have that luxury. I know the cost, and I am prepared to pay it, with or without your cooperation."

Pip remembered what Belle had said about his reputation being in as much danger as her own. "Because of your honor?" she guessed.

He gave a wary nod, seeking the words that would explain his determination to make her his bride. "When I was young, things were . . . difficult," he began carefully. "My father was but a second son, and I was his second son. I believed there was no chance I would inherit, but that didn't mean I wasn't raised knowing I had an obligation to the St. Ives name. Duty and honor were drilled into me since before I could walk, and I would die sooner than do anything that would bring disgrace upon my family. Whether you choose to accept the fact or not, we have been compromised, and as far as I am concerned, that makes you my fiancée."

Pip's bottom lip quivered at his implacable words. Arrogance she could fight—and had fought—most willingly, but she had no defense against his unswerving determination. The worst of it was she understood his reasoning, but that did not make it any easier for her to accept the truth of what he was saying. She turned the matter over in her mind, examining it as one would a shell found on the beach, searching for any way of satisfying both his honor and her own.

"Perhaps," she began carefully, "we could *pretend* to be engaged until the talk dies down. Not all engagements end in marriage, and we could—"

"No."

She raised her head at his curt refusal. "But you haven't even heard the rest of what I was about to say!" she exclaimed, her willingness to cooperate vanishing.

"I don't need to hear it to know it will not suit," Alex replied sternly. He'd been too indulgent with her, he decided, hardening his heart against the anguish in her shimmering green eyes. It was obvious she was far too emotional to deal logically with the situation, and it was up to him to take command.

"I took the liberty of retrieving this from my estate," he said, advancing on her as he withdrew a small, velvet-covered box from his breast pocket. "We may have to have it adjusted, but I am hoping it will fit. It has been in my family for generations."

Pip held her hands behind her back. "I won't wear it," she warned, backing warily away.

"You think it ostentatious?" Alex flipped open the top, revealing a pear-shaped diamond surrounded by smaller baguette stones. "How odd. I recall my grandmother wearing it with pride."

Pip collided with the edge of the tea table, halting her flight. "It is a lovely ring," she said, annoyed by the breathless sound to her voice. "You know perfectly well that is not what I meant."

"Then you like it?" He reached out calmly and grasped her hand.

Pip tugged frantically but could not free her hand. "Alex, I am warning you—"

"There." He slid the band easily on to her finger. "A perfect fit. That bodes well for our future, don't you agree?"

Pip gazed down at her hand, held tightly in his own, and for a traitorous moment she found herself wishing he'd given her the ring for reasons other than necessity.

Perhaps if he'd asked her to marry him because he loved her, and not because he had to, her answer would have been different. The very thought sent panic skittering through her, and she renewed her struggles to free her hand.

"I won't wear this," she vowed, fear and confusion giving her voice a hysterical edge. "And if anyone asks if we are engaged, I shall deny everything!"

"Will you?" Alex heard the front door being thrown open, and knew their brief period of privacy was almost at an end. Using his grip on her hand, he pulled her into a strong embrace. "It won't do you any good, you know. I'll simply deny your denial, and in the end who do you think they will believe?"

His words horrified her because she knew he was right. If it came down to a choice, the *ton* would not hesitate to side with him. "Alex, if you do not let me go this very instant—"

"I am sorry, Pip," Alex interrupted, drawing her even closer as he bent his head to hers, "but this is for the best." And his lips closed over hers in a kiss of burning urgency.

She should struggle; Pip knew that as well as she knew her own name. She was a well-brought-up young lady, and well-brought-up young ladies didn't stand in meek acquiescence while a notorious rake assaulted them. But even as these thoughts filled Pip's head, she found herself responding to the fierce hunger in Alex's kiss. It was like that time in the garden, she thought, her eyes closing as pleasure washed over her. She'd never experienced anything so wonderful, and for that brief moment she could think of no reason why she should protest. Giving a soft sigh, she slipped her hands around Alex's neck.

The feel of her fingers tentatively stroking his neck filled Alex with satisfaction. She was a fire burning in his arms, and the passion she offered was a balm to his soul. It would work out, he promised himself, deepening the kiss hungrily. So long as they shared such desire, it would all work out in the end.

"Phillipa!"

The shocked voice coming from the doorway recalled Alex to his senses. He reluctantly lifted his mouth from Pip's. He allowed himself the luxury of one brief look at her sweetly flushed face before turning to confront Mrs. Beachton.

"You may be the first to wish us happiness, ma'am," he said, slipping a possessive arm about Pip's waist. "Phillipa has consented to become my wife."

Mrs. Beachton's look of shocked disapproval vanished in a twinkling. "Then it is true?" she cried in delight, abandoning her dignity as she raced across the room to embrace a stunned Pip. "Oh, my dears, this has made me the happiest of women!"

Pip endured her aunt's exuberant embrace, too shocked to do anything else. It was like being in the midst of a dream where everything was topsy-turvy and she was expected to set them right, she thought somewhat dazedly.

"You little scamp." Mrs. Beachton was laughing as she pressed a kiss to Pip's cheek. "I had all but given up hope on you! And to think you denied everything when I twigged you about his lordship. Naughty, naughty."

"Aunt, I—this is not what you think," Pip stammered, finally finding her voice. "Alex and I—"

"And as for you, your lordship, don't think I've forgiven you for ignoring the formalities." Mrs. Beachton was giving Alex a playful scold. "It was very bad of you to send the announcement to the papers before seeking my permission. You would have looked exceedingly foolish had I said no."

"I was counting upon your kind heart to forgive a former soldier his eagerness," Alex said smoothly, his arm still clasped about Pip's waist. "I was so delighted when Phillipa said yes, I couldn't wait to announce it to the world."

Pip came to life at that. "I did *not* say yes!" she cried indignantly. "I said no, and I am still saying no! I am *not* engaged to you!"

"Oh ho, and I suppose that's not his engagement ring you've got on your finger, either." Mrs. Beachton chortled with obvious delight. " 'Tis plain as pudding the pair of you was meant for each other. Now," she rushed on before Pip could refute this, "we must be practical. We'll want a London wedding, of course. Our local chapel is quite suitable. Small, but perfectly charming. We could—"

"Aunt Morwenna, will you please listen to me?" Pip had managed to free herself from Alex's grip and was glaring at her aunt with something akin to panic in her voice. "I am *not* marrying Alex!"

The look of motherly indulgence faded from Mrs. Beachton's face. "Yes, you are," she said in a voice that showed she was still very much the general's wife. "I did not wish to say anything, since the viscount has decided to do the honorable thing, but I am aware of the wretched bet. And after the announcement in this morning's paper, I think it best that you consider yourself an engaged woman."

Pip whirled on Alex, feeling like a fox surrounded by yapping dogs. "This is all your doing!" she accused furiously, tears beginning to pool in her eyes. "And I *won't* marry you; I *won't!*" And with that, she picked up her skirts and fled from the room, unable to bear another moment of his company.

Lord Colford was waiting for Alex when he returned home, and he wasted little time in getting to the reason for his visit. "Is this true?" he asked, handing Alex a copy of the morning paper.

"Why?" Alex asked, crossing the room to the cellarette to pour himself a hefty glass of brandy. "Have you come to offer us your felicitations?"

"No, I came because I didn't believe a word of it," Marcus returned with an angry frown. I thought at first that Toby was making mischief again, but he denied any knowledge of it when I confronted him. Said it wasn't in his 'lyrical style,' whatever the devil that means."

Alex's lips lifted in a half-smile. "Doubtlessly because it didn't rhyme," he said, and went on to inform the earl of his heir's literary ambitions.

"Lord, the cub is an imbecile." Marcus groaned, accepting the glass of brandy Alex held out to him. "Perhaps my man of business is right to press marriage upon me; it would be beyond disastrous if he were to accede to the title. Ah well, if the announcement was none of his doing, then it must have been Reginald Kingsford. It seems you were right to mistrust his motives."

Alex settled into his favorite chair, idly swinging his booted foot as he took a deep sip of the fiery brandy. "Much as I dislike Kingsford, I really cannot allow him to be repeatedly blamed for something he did not do. My announcement may not have been up to your cousin's exacting standards, but I like to think it was effective."

Marcus choked on his mouthful of wine. "Your announcement?" he gasped, his russet eyebrows arching in disbelief. "Do you mean to say you sent it in? You are engaged to the bluestocking?"

Alex did not care for this slighting reference to Pip, and his displeasure was obvious in his cool voice. "Her name is Miss Lambert, at least until she becomes my viscountess," he informed Marcus, his blue eyes narrowing. "I will thank you to remember that."

Marcus hastily set down his glass. "Believe me, Alex, I did not mean to give offense," he said, holding both hands up in a placating manner. "The lady has my most sincere admiration if she is willing to take on a reprobate like you. It is just that I am somewhat amazed. When we last spoke you told me you had no interest whatsoever in Miss Lambert."

Alex gave an uncomfortable shrug and took another sip of brandy. "Things change," he muttered, his eyes flicking away from Marcus's sharp gray gaze.

"So they do, but not this drastically," Marcus returned bluntly, leaning forward in his chair. "Would you care to tell me what is really going on here, and if there is anything I can do to help?"

Alex heaved a heavy sigh and gave Marcus a succinct account of last Saturday's events, carefully omitting any reference to the bet or Miss Portham's minor role in the drama. "So you see," he concluded, "I have no choice but to marry her. Kingsford might be sufficiently frightened of me to hold his tongue now, but once his bruises fade his memory may fade as well, and it would take but one word from him or his bitch of a sister to destroy Pip's name forever."

"You could always call him out and be done with it," Marcus suggested, his voice filled with contempt for Kingsford. "Dead men are notoriously silent, and from what I have observed you would be doing the world a favor."

"True, but that still leaves Miss Kingsford, and a gentleman cannot shoot a lady, however much she might deserve it."

"That is so, and more's the pity." Marcus's mouth twisted in a wry smile. "I remember her from a few Seasons back. She is a vindictive and spiteful shrew. Ah well, so when is the wedding to be? I believe your announcement mentioned it would take place at your country estate?"

"Yes, but Phillipa's aunt, Mrs. Beachton, has indicated she would prefer the ceremony be held here in the city," Alex said, recalling the older woman's excited plans. "Personally I don't give a tinker's damn where it is done, so long as it is done quickly."

"What about Miss Lambert?" Marcus asked, looking puzzled. "Surely she must have expressed some preference in the matter?"

"Actually"—Alex's eyes took on a rueful gleam—"that is what you might call a sticky subject. The lady refuses to admit she is my fiancée."

Marcus's eyes grew wide. "Good heavens, she cannot be so foolish as that!" he exclaimed, looking properly shocked. "She must see that there is no other choice."

"Actually, she sees no such thing," Alex said, relieved that Marcus agreed with him. "In fact, the last I saw of her she was announcing rather dramatically that she would never marry me, and dashing out of the room as if I was the devil himself come to claim her."

"What do you intend doing about it?" Marcus asked, his expression grim.

"Why, marry her, of course." Alex lifted his glass in a mocking salute. "You forget I was in the army for almost twelve years, and if I learned anything in that time, it was how to conduct a campaign. Listen carefully, Colford, this is what I want you to do . . ."

Eleven

The flowers arrived the next morning, accompanied by the most stunning diamond and pearl necklace and earrings Pip had ever seen. There was no note with the magnificent tribute, but Pip didn't need one to know who'd sent them. After giving the necklace a longing look, she snapped the case closed and tossed it on the tea table.

"And he has the nerve of accusing Belle of trying to buy a husband," she muttered, her green eyes showing the effects of a sleepless night spent crying. "If he thinks I can be swayed by a few paltry trinkets such as these, then he is even more foolish than I first thought him."

"I would hardly call the St. Ives's pearls a 'paltry trinket.'" Mrs. Beachton had picked up the jewelry case and was eagerly examining the contents. "Doubtlessly he means for you to wear them when he introduces you as his wife."

"Then he will wait forever," Pip vowed darkly, "because I shan't marry him regardless of how many jewels he fobs off on me."

Mrs. Beachton sighed and set the pearls down. "Phillipa," she began in the tone of one weary of arguing, "we have been over this and over this. How many times must I tell you that there is nothing left to be done? His lordship is trying to do the honorable thing, and I for one fail to see why you insist upon fighting him. It's not as if the man was an ogre, after all."

Pip bit her lip, wishing she could tell her aunt that this was precisely the problem. Had Alex been reprehensible in either appearance or conduct, then she wouldn't feel torn in a dozen different directions. "Perhaps not to you," she said, turning away lest her aunt see the indecision in her eyes, "but then, you aren't the one being forced to marry him, are you?"

"I only wish that I were," Mrs. Beachton answered with surprising candidness. "A man as honorable and well-heeled as he is handsome would be a prize catch for any female, and you ought to be thanking your lucky stars he has chosen you."

"He didn't 'choose' me, Aunt," Pip reminded her with a bitter smile. "He is stuck with me. A great difference, I am sure you will agree."

"Only because you choose to make it so," Mrs. Beachton replied tartly, wondering how any female as intelligent as her niece could be so singularly foolish. It was all her late brother-in-law's fault, she decided, feeling aggrieved. Had be not tried to browbeat his daughter into submission, she wouldn't be so mulishly stubborn now. Well, no matter. She didn't intend to let the gel throw away the best thing that had ever happened to her out of false pride. She was a general's widow, after all, and if there was one thing she had learned, it was the need for decisive action.

"Well, you may sit about all day and lament if you want to," she said, rising to her feet, "but I have better things to do. My ladies' group meets this afternoon, and I need to be going."

"But Aunt—" Pip protested, shocked by her aunt's cavalier attitude. "What about St. Ives?"

"What about him?" Mrs. Beachton feigned disinterest. "He is your fiancé, and so far as I am concerned he is your responsibility. Do what you will about him."

And she swept from the room, leaving an open-mouthed Pip staring after her.

After her aunt's defection Pip spent an unprofitable morning weighing her options. She was no closer to reaching a decision when the callers began arriving. Ladies she could not remember meeting suddenly declared themselves her bosom friend, eagerly demanding all the details of her engagement to Alex. When she cautiously tried to explain there was no engagement, she was met with indulgent laughter, and after the first few attempts she threw up her hands in defeat. She sat in stiff silence, a pained smile on her lips as she accepted their congratulations and endured their heavy-handed interrogation.

Things were little better when she fled to Belle's house for safety. Members of her own small circle were there, and they all seemed quite pleased with the news of her coming nuptials. Even Eliza Moorehead, whom Pip had always regarded as big a misanthropist as herself, pronounced her satisfaction with the match, adding with a wink that if a female had to shackle herself to some brute of a man, then at least he should be a handsome and titled brute.

When the others finally departed, Pip turned to Belle, but if she expected to find any sympathy she was soon disappointed.

"You must not be so hard on society, Pip," Belle said, her tone remonstrative. "Most people believe what it is convenient for them to believe. And in a way you should be grateful St. Ives has acted so swiftly in claiming you as his fiancée. Now that you are to be a viscountess, all talk of that foolish bet has ceased. No one would dare utter a word against a St. Ives."

"I realize that," Pip agreed, a painful lump in her throat, "but that doesn't mean I enjoy all this. I really don't wish to marry him, you know."

"I know." Belle's eyes softened. "But for now I think it would be best if you let the engagement stand."

"Perhaps." It was an admission Pip never thought to make, but she did not see that she had any other choice. She was simply too tired and too confused to continue fighting what seemed to be a lost battle. And she was honest enough to admit that she no longer knew whom she was fighting—Alexander, or herself.

"How did things go between you and St. Ives after I left?" Belle asked, picking up her teacup and settling back in her chair. It was late afternoon, and sunlight streamed through the mullioned windows, bathing the gold and cream parlor in a soft, burnished light. "I surmise the two of you did not come to blows?"

"Oh no, he merely stuck this gaudy thing on my finger and pronounced us engaged," Pip grumbled, offering her hand for Belle's inspection. "I don't know why I haven't taken the silly thing off, except that I am terrified of losing it."

"Yes, it looks quite valuable," Belle agreed, dutifully admiring the diamond ring.

"You should see the set of pearls that arrived this morning," Pip continued, stroking the largest stone with the tip of her finger. "Aunt was in alt, but I cannot imagine wearing anything so costly. I mean to return them the very next time I see Alex."

Belle noted her familiar use of the viscount's name with a secret smile. "Speaking of his lordship, what has he to say for himself?" she asked casually. "Did he send you a *billet doux* along with the pearls?"

"He did not." Even under torture Pip would not admit to the disappointment she had felt. "I've neither seen nor heard from the man since yesterday. For someone who claims to be so set to marry me, he has been rather conspicuous by his absence."

"Mmm," Belle answered, seeking refuge behind her teacup. She wisely turned the discussion to other matters, and they soon fell into an easy conversation. They were dissecting a recent political tract when the door opened and a tall woman with bright red hair came striding into the room, a large book cradled in her hands.

"Here it is," she said, her voice surprisingly melodic. "I knew I had seen it on your shelves."

"So you did." Belle accepted the massive volume with a smile. "Thank you, Miranda."

"What is it?" Pip leaned closer for a better look.

"The Life of Plato in the original Greek," the other woman answered, retrieving the book from Belle and showing it to Pip. "Miss Portham and I were discussing Plato and Socrates earlier today, and when I mentioned this particular work, she said she was certain she did not have it."

"And she was equally insistent that I did," Belle agreed, giving her a warm smile. "It pains me to admit I am so unfamiliar with the contents of my own library. But enough of Plato; allow me to introduce the two of you. Pip, this is my newest companion, Miss Miranda Cates. Miranda, I should like you to meet Miss Phillipa Lambert, my very good friend."

Miranda turned knowing hazel eyes on Pip. "Ah, you're the one who bagged a viscount," she said, with no hint of malice in the smile she bestowed upon Pip. "Well, I wish you joy of him. Despite what the wags may say, reformed rakes seldom make the best of husbands. They just go on with their rakehell ways, or so I have always observed. Now if you will pardon me, I had best be returning Plato to his niche. Your library is in a dreadful shambles, if you do not mind my saying so, Miss Portham, but I will soon have it set to rights. You can't have more than a few hundred volumes," and she departed as abruptly as she had appeared.

"Now you can see why I despair of ever finding her a post," Belle remarked to Pip when they were alone again. "Poor Miranda hasn't the foggiest notion how a proper companion is to behave, and is inclined to speak her mind regardless of the consequences."

"She is a quiz," Pip agreed, smiling at the thought of

the lively redhead forced into the servile role of a companion. "What do you intend doing with her?"

"Well, much as I would like to keep her with me, I am afraid it would never do. We are both too strong-willed to exist in perpetual harmony, and, in any case, with Julia making her bows next year, I shall be much too busy. Still, I suppose I can keep her on until I find her something. A governess post, perhaps. She is frightfully well-educated."

They were still discussing various possibilities for employment when the door opened and the subject under discussion poked her head inside the room. "Oh, I forgot to tell you, Miss Portham, but two gentlemen have arrived and are asking to see both you and Miss Lambert."

"Who are they?" Belle asked, her brow wrinkling as she tried to remember whether or not she had been expecting any callers.

"The viscount of St. Ives and the earl of something or other," Miranda answered with a disinterested shrug. "I think he must be related to the poet because their names were similar."

"Which poet?" This time it was Pip who provided the prompting, her spirits lifting at the thought of seeing Alex again.

"The one who wrote that Gothic monstrosity about the seagull," Miranda said, her finely arched brows gathering in a disapproving frown. "I think he was trying to ape Shakespeare's *The Tempest*, although he did a very poor job of it, if you want my opinion."

It took Belle very little time to realize Miranda was talking about Coleridge and "The Ancient Mariner," and from there she made the obvious connection to her nemesis. "Colford?" she demanded in a disbelieving voice. "The earl of Colford is here? In my house?"

"That's his name." Miranda nodded her head. "Shall I tell Gilman to show them in?"

Belle's eyes took on a militant sparkle that Pip recognized all too well. She fully expected to hear her issue a curt order that the earl be thrown out on to the street, and was shocked when Belle said, "Please. Oh, and ask Cook to bring us some fresh tea. This pot needs freshening."

"All right." Miranda pulled the door shut again, and Pip turned to Belle. "I don't believe this," she said, making no attempt to hide her astonishment. "You're offering refreshment to *Colford?*"

"What other choice have I? I can scarce toss the wretch out, however much I should like to. Besides"— her full lips tightened in annoyance—"I much doubt he would leave."

That seemed more than probable, and so the two sat in uneasy silence as they waited for their guests to join them. Alex was the first through the door, and there was no faulting his smooth manner as he made a direct line to Pip's side.

"I have been looking all over London for you," he chided, his blue eyes warm as he swept her hand to his lips. "I might have known I would find you here."

"Then perhaps you ought to have looked here first," she returned, tamping down the pleasure the touch of his lips brought her. "And what do you mean you have been looking for me? Did you not enquire at my house? The staff knew I was at Belle's."

So they did, which was precisely what he was doing here, Alex thought, hiding his irritation behind an intimate smile. He had only been speaking figuratively, a fact any lady with an ounce of sense would have realized. He might have guessed Pip would choose to take him literally. "No matter, I have found you now," he said, slipping into the chair beside her with practiced ease. "My curricle is outside, and I am hoping you and Miss Portham will accompany me on a drive about the park."

"I don't know," Pip began hesitantly, thinking how

very lovely a ride sounded. "We really should avoid being alone again together, and—"

"But you shan't be alone," the earl of Colford interrupted, his gray eyes dancing as he made his bows first to Belle and then to Pip. "You shall be well chaperoned by the redoubtable Miss Portham, and I shall be along to chaperone her. What could be more harmless than four old friends enjoying a turn about the park?"

"Old friends, your lordship?" Belle arched her blond eyebrows in cool defiance.

"Old enemies, then," he amended, dismissing her attempts at a set-down with a mocking smile. "Besides, a drive in the fresh air is just the thing to put the color back in your lovely cheeks." He reached out and flicked a teasing finger down the curve of Belle's cheek.

She batted his hand away with an irritated scowl. "I should not talk of *cheek* if I were you, sir," she retorted, her voice vibrating with anger. "And you are mad if you think I mean to climb into a carriage with you."

"Not a carriage, a curricle," Colford corrected with that same maddening smile. "And you wouldn't be so cruel as to deprive your dear friend of a ride, would you? She and St. Ives may be engaged, but even engaged couples must observe the niceties. Is that not so, Miss Lambert?" He turned toward Pip.

Pip felt like an army being attacked on two fronts. She didn't see how she could disagree with the audacious earl without making it seem as if she wanted to be alone with Alex. That she did want to be alone with him was beside the point, and in the end she gave the only answer she felt she could give.

"Please do come, Arabella," she said through gritted teeth, missing the triumphant look that flashed between Alex and the earl. "I should welcome your company."

"Very well." Belle, too intent on clinging to her icy demeanor to pay the men much note, had also missed the silent exchange. "If you will excuse me, I shall go and get my cloak."

In her absence Pip acted as hostess, pouring each man his cup when the tea arrived and offering them a selection of delicacies. Alex watched her over the rim of his cup, his eyes filled with satisfaction as he said, "You do that most gracefully, Phillipa. I cannot wait to see you pouring tea in our house."

The teapot wavered precariously in Pip's hand before she managed to set it down. Several replies to this outrageous remark leapt readily to mind, but in the end she decided to go with the one she deemed the safest. "Thank you, your lordship," she said, her eyes fixed firmly on the silver tea set in front of her.

Alex exchanged another knowing look with Marcus. Things were working out just as he'd planned, he decided complaisantly. All he had to do was keep Pip off her feet and confused, and he would have her in front of the altar before she knew what was happening. Such harassing maneuvers had worked wonders on the peninsula, and he could see no reason why they wouldn't work just as well now.

Thirty minutes later the two couples were tooling toward the park. Because he wanted the chance to converse with Pip, Alex had his coachman drive, rather than handling the ribbons himself, as was his custom. He and Pip sat with their backs to the horses, and he waited until he was certain Marcus had Miss Portham sufficiently distracted before turning to Pip.

"I know your aunt mentioned a town wedding," he said with an encouraging smile, "but I've yet to hear your opinion. For myself, I would prefer being married from my own home as my predecessors have always done, but naturally I shall bow to you in the matter."

Such brass left Pip bereft of speech, but only temporarily. She drew herself up and sent him a scathing look. "If you bow to *my* wishes in this matter, your lordship, there won't *be* a wedding," she retorted, careful to keep her voice low-pitched.

"Ah, then you prefer the country, too," he said, nodding agreeably. "Good, you can see how well-suited we are."

"I never said any such thing, you beast!" Despite her best efforts, Pip's voice rose several octaves. "How dare you put words in my mouth!"

"London it shall be." Alex reached out and gave her hand a pat. "I shall place my staff at your disposal so that you and your aunt may arrange everything between you."

"Oh, it is no use talking to you!" Pip charged, jerking her hand from beneath his and moving as far from him as the narrow seat would permit. "You are determined to have your own way in this!"

"Nonsense." He shifted closer, his hard thigh pressing against hers. "I have just proven how compliant I mean to be. Now that that is settled, I thought we might discuss tomorrow evening."

"What of it?" Pip's eyes strayed to the other side of the curricle, noting with interest Belle's bright cheeks and flashing eyes. Evidently Colford was proving as big a plague to her friend as Alex was to her.

"I thought we might go to Almack's. It will be our first formal appearance since our engagement was announced, and I am desirous that we make the correct entrance," Alex said, nodding an acknowledgement to a passing acquaintance. "Did the pearls arrive?"

"This morning," Pip admitted, still smarting over his comment about a "correct" entrance.

"Good. Then you will wear them with that lovely yellow dress of yours, the one you wore our first night at Thorn Hill."

She bristled at the audacity of his request. "You would make yourself my lady's maid, sir?" she asked, injecting as much sarcasm as she could into the question.

"If I must," Alex replied with the condescension worthy of a king. "It is a husband's right to choose his lady's clothing if he so chooses."

"But you are *not* my husband," Pip pointed out with a defiant tilt of her chin.

"Not yet," he agreed, his eyes meeting hers with unexpected force. "But I will be, Pip, and soon. And when I do, you may make very sure that I shall waste little time claiming my husbandly privileges. All of them," he added after a meaningful pause.

Pip's cheeks burned with color as his meaning hit her. He did not mean . . . he could not mean . . . she simply wasn't the sort of female men thought of in that fashion. Her own father had pronounced her dull and plain, and she had always believed him. A man like Alex, who could have his pick of any woman, could never really want her—could he?

She allowed this tantalizing prospect to nibble at her conscience as the curricle turned off Hertford Street and into the parade and pageantry that was Hyde Park. It was almost five o'clock, and the narrow drive was filled with opulent carriages and their elegantly dressed occupants. Ladies in their finest muslins and silks flirted with handsome men sitting astride high-strung stallions.

Alex was greeted by several friends, and Pip was ashamed that she was taking perverse pleasure in the attention they were drawing. After spending most of her life on the edges of society, she found it rather exciting to be at the very center of things. They had just completed their second circuit of the park and were discussing starting for home when a blond-haired man sitting atop a glossy black came riding up to greet them.

"Ah, St. Ives, so it is you," he drawled, his teeth flashing in a mocking grin. "What an unexpected delight to find you here."

"Hollingsworth." Alex's voice was stiff with civility as he recognized the notorious marquess of Hollingsworth. The man was a known gamester and mischief-maker, and Alex wondered glumly why he had chosen to honor them with his dubious attentions.

If the marquess was at all offended by Alex's brusqueness, he gave no indication of it. Instead he turned to Pip, his smile mocking as he lifted his hat to her. "And the lovely bride," he murmured, his voice heavy with innuendo. "Pray accept my felicitations on your coming marriage."

"Thank you, your lordship, that is most kind of you," she responded, vividly aware of Alex bristling beside her. It was obvious he disliked the marquess, and she was more than willing to follow his lead in this.

"Not at all, Miss Lambert." Hollingsworth's manner bordered on the insolent. "You must know your engagement is the talk of London. Prinny is beside himself with amusement. He is *such* a romantic, and it pleases him to think you met as a result of his ball. In fact, I heard him say he was thinking of making the pair of you his special guests of honor—a rather singular distinction, you know."

"But we aren't attending His Highness's ball," she protested, her brows wrinkling in confusion.

Hollingsworth's blue eyes grew wide with mock dismay. "You aren't? How very odd. I had heard his lordship had already sent in your acceptance to the prince."

Alex's gloved hands clenched into tight fists at the stunned look on Pip's face. He'd meant to inform her of his decision later, after he'd soothed her fears regarding their engagement, and he could cheerfully murder Hollingsworth for spoiling his plans. "We shall discuss this later, Phillipa," he said, his voice tight with control.

"But Alex—"

"Oh dear, have I let the cat out of the bag?" the marquess asked, all but licking his lips in malicious delight as his eyes flicked from Pip's stunned expression to Alex's controlled mask.

Pip was the first to recover, her pride rising to the

fore. Not for anything would she allow this obnoxious coxcomb the gratification of knowing he had hurt her, she vowed, pinning a swift smile on her lips.

"So that is why you gave me the St. Ives pearls!" she exclaimed, turning to Alex with a laugh. "Silly man, why did you not tell me?"

"Because I wanted it to be a surprise, my love," he said, his years as a soldier allowing him to accept her performance without turning so much as a hair. "Am I to take it you are pleased?"

"Pleased? I am speechless," Pip replied with decided irony. She turned back to Hollingsworth, her smile still in place. "You must inform His Royal Highness that we are deeply grateful for the honor he has shown us," she said with the cool aplomb she had often seen Belle display. "I daresay it is not every engaged couple that has so royal a host."

The marquess's look of petulant anger was almost comical. For a moment Pip thought he meant to throw a childish tantrum, but at the last second he seemed to regain control over himself. "I am sure they do not," he snapped in a decidedly waspish tone, his hands tightening on the reins of his mount. "Miss Portham, Lord Colford," he belatedly acknowledged Belle's and Marcus's presence before wheeling his horse around and galloping away.

"What a thoroughly unpleasant man," Belle remarked in the tense silence that followed his departure. "A particular friend of yours, is he not?" She turned to Marcus with a challenging look.

Marcus picked up the hint at once, understanding that she was giving Alex and Miss Lambert time to recover themselves. "Oh, we are bosom beaus," he drawled in his most provocative manner, his arms folding across his chest. "But I must say I am surprised to find you disclaiming any liking for him. After all, he is one of those loose-living Whigs you seem to admire."

While Belle spiritedly defended her political friends,

Pip found herself on the verge of throwing a tantrum of her own. Learning that Alex planned for them to attend the prince's ball had come as a profound shock, although now that she thought about it, she wondered why she should be surprised. Only look at the way he had announced their engagement, sending notices to the papers even after her vehement refusal. Well, she decided, her eyes shimmering with indignation, if he thought he could dragoon her into this as well, he was sorely mistaken. She had evidently been far too accommodating, and it was time she reminded him that she was not his to lead about like a brainless child.

Alex saw the anger on Pip's expressive face and silently cursed Hollingsworth. The devil take the bastard for his malicious tongue, he thought furiously. Were it not for the scandal, he would gladly put a bullet in him, but as it was there was nothing he could do except try to repair the damage that had been done. Having come this far, he was not about to let a preening dandy undo all his hard work.

Bell and Marcus continued their half-serious, half-playful squabbling as the curricle made its way back to Belle's home in Mayfair. When they pulled up in front of her house, Marcus got down as well. "I believe I shall walk to my club from here," he said, his tone light. "Arguing with Miss Portham has upset my delicate constitution, and I must walk a bit if I mean to recover my equanimity."

"Ha! More like 'tis the brandy you Corinthians imbibe so freely that has upset your nerves!" Belle shot back, loosing her icy dignity enough to glower at him. The glower faded as she turned to Pip.

"Shall we be seeing you this evening, then?" she asked, her eyes worried as they studied her friend's strained features.

"Certainly, her aunt shall be chaperoning us," Alex answered before Pip could open her mouth. "We shall look forward to seeing you."

Belle looked as if there were more she would like to say, but a gentle poke from Marcus had her murmuring her farewells. Pip managed a strangled goodbye of her own, and the curricle began moving again.

They continued in silence for several blocks, then, just as Pip was getting ready to let fly with her temper, Alex said, "I know you are doubtlessly itching to ring a peal over my head, but I would ask that you control yourself until we reach your aunt's house. We are attracting enough attention as it is for appearing without a chaperone."

Pip shot him a meaningful glare, but other than a lofty sniff she did not deign to answer him. She waited until the drawing room door had closed behind them before turning on him in a rage.

"How *dare* you tell the prince we would attend his tiresome ball?" she demanded, although she was careful to keep her voice low-pitched lest the servants be listening at the keyholes. "You must know I have no desire to go there!"

"Desire and duty are not always the same thing, Phillipa," he declared coolly, determined to keep his temper. "It will do us no harm to attend, and now that His Highness has chosen us as his guests of honor, I do not see that there is much we can do. One does not refuse what amounts to a royal summons."

Pip knew that, and it irked her no end that she could not refute him. She tried a different tack instead. "I still say we should not go," she argued with renewed anger. "What of the bet? If I do go with you, it will look as if you are using our engagement to win the silly thing!"

"Then let it," he answered calmly. "What do we care what small minds may think?"

Pip stopped pacing, her eyes wide with confusion as she whirled around to face him. "But the gossip—" she began weakly, not understanding what was happening between them. She should be furious—she *was* furious—and yet there was something in Alex's sapphire-blue eyes that turned her fury into an emotion she was too frightened to acknowledge.

"I told you, our engagement has put an end to all the gossip," he said, his voice deep as he walked up to her and caught her icy hands in his. "You are to be my wife, the Viscountess St. Ives, and any man who dares mentions your name with anything other than the utmost respect is courting death. I am a man who knows how to guard his own, Phillipa, and you may be very sure I shall take exceptional care of you. You need have no fears on that score."

Something deep in Pip's heart shattered. The wall she had always kept between herself and the fear of yet another rejection came tumbling down, and she was finally able to accept the truth she had so vehemently avoided. The admission was on her lips, but the fears and uncertainties of a lifetime kept her from uttering it. Instead she sought refuge in humor, her eyes taking on a teasing sparkle.

"And what of the ladies?" she asked with a light laugh, making no attempt to free her hands from his. "Would you call them out as well?"

Alex had seen the emotion in Pip's green eyes, and he wondered what she was thinking. He had always considered himself to be impervious to the whims and moods of other people, and yet of late he often found himself lying in bed at night and brooding over the state of Pip's mind. He pretended it was because he needed to know what she was thinking and feeling so that he could control her, but he knew now that that was a lie. He was vulnerable to Pip in a way he had never been vulnerable to another human being, and the realization left him dazed. Shaking off his inner musings, he summoned up an answering smile to match hers.

"I have other ways of dealing with tattling ladies," he assured her, lifting their joined hands to his lips for a kiss. "In the meanwhile, I want our engagement accepted by everyone, including you, and our appearance at the prince's ball will see to that."

"Oh?" Pip's heart raced at the feel of his warm lips brushing over her hands. "And do you really think I am so easily led as that?"

Alex's lips curved in a rueful smile. "I think even you, my love, would draw the line at offending a prince. Now, have I your word that you will behave yourself like a lady and attend the ball with me?"

"Have I any other choice?"

"No, although I am probably slitting my own throat by admitting as much." Alex released one of her hands to caress her cheek. "Go with me, Pip. Show the world that you are truly my fiancée."

Pip's lips parted as his thumb moved back and forth across them in a sure, even stroke. "B–but the wager—" she stammered, her eyes closing as pleasure washed over her.

"There is something you need to know about that damned bet." Alex's voice was deep with desire at the sight of Pip's lips parting beneath his touch.

"Wh–what about it?" Pip was finding it difficult to think over the tumultuous pounding of her heart.

"The day we returned from Thorn Hill I went to White's and settled my account."

Pip's eyes flew open in disbelief. "What?"

He gave a nod, pleased she understood what he was implying. "I settled the account," he repeated, drawing her into his arms. "I told the bookmaker I had lost and paid up as befits a gentleman. So you see, there is no bet. At least, not as far as I am concerned."

"But why didn't you tell me this sooner?" Pip gave his broad shoulders an angry push. "You must know I thought that was the only reason you persisted in offering for me!"

"No man likes explaining himself to anyone, least of all a woman." Alex laughed at her ferocious scowl. "Besides, you know I offered for you because I had no other choice. Now, stop throwing arguments at my head and give me a kiss. An engaged man is allowed some liberties, you know."

Pip scowled up at him for another moment and then she gave him a sunny smile, her arms stealing about his neck. "Oh, very well, you beast," she said, closing her mind to the pain he had caused by reminding her of the true reasons for their coming marriage. "But only a small kiss, mind. As you are forever lecturing me, I have my reputation to think of."

Alex gave an appreciative chuckle and lowered his lips to hers, his hungry mouth telling her all the things his heart had not yet the courage to speak.

Twelve

The next two weeks were among the happiest of Pip's life. Since their first official appearance at Almack's, she and Alex had been besieged with invitations, and once her initial wariness faded she found herself enjoying the social whirl. She tried believing it was because she'd finally shaken off the last vestiges of her father's bitter disapproval, but she knew the true cause was the handsome man standing so confidently at her side. With Alex backing her, she felt there was nothing she could not endure.

Now that she could admit that she loved Alex, it felt as if a great burden had been lifted from her shoulders. She knew he was the only man she could ever hope to love, and if there were any black clouds darkening the halcyon days, they were caused by the painful knowledge that he did not return that love. Oh, he liked her—and if the increasingly feverish kisses they exchanged were any indication, he desired her. But that was far from the all-consuming love she secretly craved. Still, half a loaf was better than none, and she counselled herself to remain content with that fact.

Three days before the ball at Carlton House, she was sitting in her study going over yet another pile of invitations when her aunt tapped on the door.

"Are you busy, my dear?" she asked, her expression

apologetic as she hovered on the threshold. "If so, I can always come back at some other time."

Pip realized she had been neglecting her aunt for the past several days, and sent the older woman a fond smile. "You shan't be disturbing me, ma'am, you shall be rescuing me," she said, giving the pile before her a disgusted shove. "Do please come inside and tell me how you have been."

Mrs. Beachton bustled forward, although her expression still remained anxious. "Oh, I have been fine," she assured her niece, with a smile that did not quite reach her darting eyes. "I went to that tea I mentioned last week and had a delightful time."

Pip had a vague memory of her mentioning a tea being sponsored by one of her gossiping cronies, but could remember little else. Anxious not to hurt her aunt's tender feelings, she cast about in her mind until she could come up with the name of the hostess at the tea.

"And how is Lady Branville?" she asked at last, the image of the plump, odious woman springing to life in her mind. "Still serving up other people's reputations along with the cream and the buns?"

Rather than taking her comment in the lighthearted manner in which it was intended, Mrs. Beachton took instant offense. "Really, Phillipa, I do wish you would not be so flip!" she scolded, her face turning an alarming shade of red. "It is most unbecoming in the young lady who is soon to be the viscountess St. Ives!"

Pip blinked in astonishment at her outburst. "I am sorry, Aunt Morwenna," she said, wondering if perhaps her aunt was brooding over something. "I was only funning."

"Having one's reputation shredded is hardly fit matter for a jest," the older woman insisted with a scowl. "Gossip, however well-intended, is hurtful, and I should think you of all people would know that."

Some of Pip's old deviltry raised its head, and her

eyes began sparkling with laughter. "How can gossip ever be well-intended?" she asked with a chuckle. "It would seem a contradiction in terms to me."

"Well, it is not." Her aunt's face turned an even deeper shade of red. "Sometimes people say things not to cause trouble, but to prevent it. At least, that is their intention."

"Is there not a quote about the road to hell being paved with good intentions?"

"Phillipa!"

"Oh, calm yourself, Aunt." Pip gave up twitting her aunt and sent her another smile. "I am sure neither you nor the countess would ever say a single word to cause anyone a moment's pain. Now, enough of that. What do you think about our plans for this evening? Will you be joining us at the Heathtons'?"

"Of course," Mrs. Beachton replied with a good-natured grumble. "I am your chaperone, after all, and you and St. Ives can hardly go about alone."

"That is so," Pip agreed, wistfully thinking of the day when she and Alex could dispense with such tiresome necessities. She and her aunt fell into an easy discussion of her wardrobe, and were debating the merits of the latest fashions out of Bond Street when her aunt suddenly said, "Phillipa, do you truly believe gossipers go to hell?"

"I beg your pardon?"

"Gossipers," Mrs. Beachton repeated, her brows gathering in a worried frown. "Do you believe they languish in the flames of eternal damnation?"

Such a theological question left Pip speechless for a few moments. "I suppose so," she said at last. "With their tongues plucked from their mouths with fiery tongs, according to Dante. Why do you ask?" she queried, unable to resist a final tease. "Do you fear such everlasting punishment?"

To her astonishment the older woman actually looked frightened. "I have sometimes wagged my tongue when

I would have been better advised holding it," she admitted, wringing her hands in obvious distress.

Pip took instant pity on her and gave her hand a loving pat. "I wouldn't worry, Aunt Morwenna," she soothed. "I am sure God has better things to do with His time than fret over every misspoken word."

"Do you think so?" Her aunt seemed pathetically eager for reassurance.

"Beyond question." Pip gave her that reassurance with a laugh. "And even if I am wrong and you should go to hell for so paltry a cause, at least you would have the comfort of knowing you will be in the best of company. Half of the *ton* will be there with you!"

"You are looking particularly lovely this evening, my sweet," Alex commented several hours later as he led Pip off the dance floor. "Have I mentioned how much I enjoy seeing you in yellow?"

"I believe you may have mentioned it, your lordship," Pip responded with a demure smile, her cheeks flushed as much from the warmth of his compliment as from the exertions of the waltz. She thought of the gown for the prince's ball that had been delivered that afternoon. Fashioned of brilliant yellow silk, it was quite the most expensive gown she had ever owned, but the feeling she got when she donned the dress made it more than worth the price. In the gown, she felt like a lady who was worthy of being the next viscountess St. Ives.

"Good." Alex absentmindedly carried her hand to his lips for a kiss. "I would not have you think me behindhand in my courting." How well it was all going, he thought, nodding at an old friend from his army days. In the fortnight since he had convinced Pip to become his wife, everything had gone precisely as he had planned.

Oh, to be sure, she was still skittish on the subject, but he did not doubt but that if he was only patient with her, he would coax her around to his way of thinking. That was why he hadn't pressed her to set the date, knowing it would almost certainly send her into full flight. Tonight, however, he decided it was time he began insisting she do just that. The prince's ball was in less than two days' time, and he wanted the matter settled before then.

He saw his opportunity almost an hour later when a very flushed Pip declared herself to be roasting in the overcrowded room. Ever the gentleman, he led her out into the Heathtons' conservatory, guiding her to a secluded corner where he knew they would be unobserved.

"Feeling better?" he asked, solicitously handing her his handkerchief so that she could wipe her face.

"Much," she admitted, dabbing at her forehead with a feeling of relief. "Thank you, your lordship, for getting me out of there before I swooned from the heat."

"Not at all," he assured her, his smile intimate as he joined her on the wicker bench. "Have I not already promised to have a care for you?"

Pip realized he was talking about their conversation in her aunt's parlor. "I remember," she said, her eyes darting from his face to the large and rather ornate fern that sheltered them from the rest of the room. There was something different about him tonight, she realized, some sense of purpose she could feel emanating from him. She wondered if he was going to tell her he loved her, and her heart raced at the possibility.

Now, he told himself, relying on the instinctive sense of timing that had often meant the difference between life and death on the battlefield; he would ask her now. "Phillipa—Pip." He leaned forward and placed a finger beneath her chin, gently turning her head until he was gazing down into her wide green eyes. "You know I have nothing but the deepest regard for you—"

". . . and pay up like a man," a disembodied voice, slurred with drink, came floating from the other side of

the palms. " 'Tis plain as a pikestaff that St. Ives has
won. The stupid wench is besotted with him."

She felt Alex stiffening with fury beside her, but before he could take any action a second voice added,
". . . still say it was unsporting of St. Ives to send his
man down to wager five thousand pounds against himself the day before his engagement was announced. He
stands to make a neat twenty thousand once the accounts are settled."

"Look upon it as a dowry," the other man advised
with a drunken laugh. "Lord knows the man deserves
it; I'd want more than a mere twenty thousand to be
saddled with that she-devil for the rest of my days. Not
that St. Ives means it to go that far, o'course. Betting is
he'll break with her the day after Prinny's ball."

"Really?" The voices were moving away. "What are
the odds? I lost damned near three thousand
pounds . . ." and the voices faded into the blackness.

Pip sat as if turned to stone. In a very far corner of
her mind she recalled someone—a nanny, she
thought—telling her that eavesdroppers never heard
good of themselves. Following on that was the memory
of the last time her father had spoken to her, his voice
filled with loathing as he berated her for having concluded her second Season without attracting so much as
a single offer.

"You're a failure, the same as your worthless
mother," he'd raged, his face purpling with the strength
of his emotions. "She couldn't give me a son, and you
can't even get me a son-in-law. You're plain and stupid,
and no man will ever want you!"

"Pip, my darling, are you all right?" Alex chafed her
hand, his worried eyes riveted on her almost white face.
"You mustn't pay any attention to those bastards. The
moment I find who they are I shall call them out for
spreading such stories!"

"You . . . you wagered against yourself?" Pip managed, raising stunned eyes to his. Another story from

her childhood—that of the boy from Sparta who remained silent even while the wild fox devoured his entrails—sprang to mind, and in that moment she knew just how the lad had felt. Eaten alive by the most incredible pain, and yet unable to utter a single sound.

"My God, no!" Alex denied, going cold as fear washed over him. He could sense her slipping away, and the horror of it was he could think of no way to stop it.

"But ... but they said ..."

"They lied, damn it!" Fear gave way to panic, and he grabbed her by the shoulders. "How could you believe such a thing of me?"

"No man will ever want you," her father's words echoed in her head, drowning out the pain in Alex's voice. She felt the bile rise in her throat, and feared she would disgrace herself by becoming ill. Anger was preferable to such tearing agony, and she seized upon the emotion with single-minded desperation.

"Considering that you instigated the original wager, your lordship, how do you think?" she asked, hearing the icy fury in her voice as if from a great distance. "My congratulations, sir, for the lengths to which you will go to achieve your goals."

Alex stared down at her as if she was a stranger. "Pip, you do not know what you are saying," he said, stunned that she could believe such lies. "You are upset."

"Not so upset as you, I imagined." Pip gave a light laugh. "How very awkward to have the truth come out just as you were about to consolidate your victory."

"Consolidate my—What the devil are you talking about?" Alex scowled down at her, feeling his tenuous control on his temper slipping.

"Evidently my agreeing to this ludicrous engagement was not enough," Pip said, taking a black pride in her indifferent tone. "Was it part of the original wager to seduce me, or is that your own touch? A sort of payment for all your hard work?"

"Phillipa, I am warning you . . ."

"Ah, but I forgot, you've already been paid, haven't you?" She gave him a smile dripping with acid. "Twenty thousand pounds, wasn't it? 'Tis a pity I did not know you would sell your honor for so little as that. Rather rich for my blood, but I daresay Belle would have been willing to pay."

Alex flinched from her words as he would from a lash. He clenched his hands so tightly he felt as if the flesh would crack. "It does not matter," he said, exercising almost painful control over his emotions. "Regardless of what you have heard or what you foolishly choose to believe, you are still my fiancée, and you will be my wife. Nothing changes that, do you understand? Nothing."

The pain was becoming too great, and in a moment Pip feared she would collapse beneath it. She stumbled on legs that felt as if they were made of water. "Of course, your lordship," she said through taut lips. "I understand completely; the prince's ball hasn't occurred yet, has it?"

"The prince and his damned ball may go to the devil," Alex gritted, fighting his own need to give way to his emotions. "I meant what I said. We *will* be married."

"Will we?" She raised shock-darkened eyes to his. "Perhaps. But I would have you know this, St. Ives: If what you are saying is so and I have no choice but to marry you, then so be it. I will give you my hand, I will even give you my body, but I shall never, ever give you my heart." And with that she walked from the room, her ears deaf to his commands to return.

"Please, Phillipa, will you not eat something?" Mrs. Beachton's voice was filled with anxiety as she hovered in the doorway of Pip's bedroom. "You haven't touched a bite of food all day!"

"No, thank you, Aunt Morwenna," Pip answered, her stomach rolling at the very thought of food. "Perhaps later."

"That is what you said this morning when you refused breakfast," Mrs. Beachton replied, inching her way into the room. "Isn't it about time you told me what is really going on? Even when you are sick as a cat I've never known you to starve yourself."

Pip could answer that going without two meals hardly put her in danger of starvation, but the remark seemed more effort than she cared to make. Instead she turned back to her melancholy perusal of the rain-swept streets, hoping that if she gave no reply her aunt would grow weary of her silence and leave.

"Maybe we should have you bled," Mrs. Beachton opined, lowering herself on to the padded window bench beside Pip. " 'Tis not a practice I have ever held with, but—"

"There is no need to send for the leeches," Pip interrupted, wearily accepting that her aunt would not leave until she had the truth. "Lord St. Ives and I have had . . . a small disagreement."

Mrs. Beachton's face cleared at once. "Is that all? Heavens, child, all couples have their spats. 'Tis to be expected. Why, I remember the time the general and I all but came to blows over—"

"It was more than a 'squabble,' Aunt Morwenna," Pip interjected with a bitter laugh. "The man betrayed me."

The older woman's hands fluttered to her throat. "Never . . . never say you have anticipated your vows," she whispered, her face paling with shock. "Oh, Phillipa—"

"No, it was nothing like that," Pip hastened to assure her, "although I wonder that he did not stoop to *that* as well," and in a rush it all came out. Her discovery of

his perfidy, their quarrel; all of it. By the time she was
finished she was in tears again, and her aunt was literally white with horror.

"Dear God!" Mrs. Beachton managed in a strangled
breath. "You called St. Ives a liar?"

"He *did* lie!" Pip cried, leaping to her feet to face her
aunt with tear-washed eyes. "He has done nothing but
lie from the moment he had Lady Jersey introduce us!
He is a rake, and a scoundrel, and a—"

"But he didn't send his man to White's to place that
bet. I only said that he did so that it would make a
scandal."

The meekly whispered confession halted Pip in mid-
tirade, and as a feeling of sickness washed over her, she
turned to her aunt. *"You* started the story?"

Mrs. Beachton nodded miserably. "I was afraid you
would refuse him," she said, her brimming eyes fixed
on the knotted handkerchief she clutched in her hands.
"You are so willful at times, there is no telling what
you might do. But I knew—or at least I hoped—you
wasn't so big a gudgeon that you would fly in the very
face of convention. I–I thought that if I made a bigger
scandal than already existed, you would see that marrying his lordship was the wisest course to follow, the
only course to follow. I only wanted to help." She
ended with an unhappy little sigh.

"Oh, Aunt Morwenna." Upset as she was, Pip could
not remain immune to the pain in her aunt's voice. She
stopped her restless pacing and hurried to the distraught
woman's side. "So this is what you meant by your talk
of well-intended gossip," she said, giving her back a
comforting pat.

Mrs. Beachton nodded again. "It was a p–plan,"
she stammered, vigorously blowing her nose. "My
late husband was always telling me I ought to have a
plan."

Pip murmured a few soothing words, even as her

mind wrestled with the dilemma of what she should do next. She would have to apologize to Alex, that much was obvious; she only hoped that he would forgive her. She knew how proud he could be, and how very dear he held his honor. She winced as she recalled the raw pain in his voice as he denied any knowledge of that second wager. How could she have doubted him?

". . . will hate me," she heard her aunt proclaim with a heart-wrenching sob. "And I do not blame him. I am a wicked, foolish old woman, and I deserve to be eternally punished for my folly."

"Don't be silly, Aunt. Of course you do *not* deserve to be punished, and certainly not for all of eternity." Pip pushed thoughts of Alex from her mind and set about comforting her aunt. "I've already told you that God will understand."

"God? I was speaking of the viscount!" Mrs. Beachton dabbed at her bleary eyes. "God I know will forgive me, for He is God. But what of St. Ives? I have blackened his name before all of society. How can he be expected to forgive me that?"

Pip gave her another pat. "If I have learned nothing else of his lordship in these last weeks, it is that he is a man with a great sense of honor and duty," she said, conveniently forgetting her previous accusations. "I am sure once he understands your . . . er . . . reasons, he will be more than willing to forgive you." Her lips formed into her first smile of the day. "Doubtlessly he will consider it his duty to do so."

A look of cautious hope stole over Mrs. Beachton's face. "Do you think so?" she asked cautiously. "I recall my husband once mentioning he has the most dreadful temper . . ."

"He is the veriest lamb," Pip lied for all she was worth. "And as I said, he is a man who understands the necessity of doing one's duty."

"Yes, he would, wouldn't he?" Mrs. Beachton nibbled thoughtfully on her finger. "And I *was* only doing my duty by you when I told that plumper. It's not as if I was being malicious, like some people I could name."

Pip found a moment to be grateful for her aunt's ability to twist reality to suit her needs. In the next moment, the older woman would be denying any wrongdoing at all. "I shall write Alex at once," Pip promised, rising from the window bench and making her way to her desk. "It was very wrong of me to have doubted him."

"Yes, it was." Mrs. Beachton gave her a reproving look as she too rose to her feet. "You must learn to be more supportive of your fiancé, my dear. It will make life far less taxing for you once you are married."

"If you say so, ma'am." Pip tested the nub of her quill on her thumb, wondering how one set about humbling oneself on paper. It would not be the easiest letter she had ever written, she acknowledged with a sigh, but it was the most important letter of her life. She only prayed to God Alex was of a mind to read it. She'd scarce set pen to paper when she heard her aunt give a startled cry.

"Heavens, 'tis Lord St. Ives! His carriage has just pulled up in front of our house!"

Pip dropped the quill onto the top of the desk and ran to stand beside her aunt. As she had said, the familiar black and gold carriage had pulled to a halt on the busy street, and even as they watched, Alex climbed down, disdaining the help of the liveried footman who had come dashing up to assist him. Even from the safety of her vantage point, Pip felt a thrill of apprehension when she saw the closed, set look on his face. He did not look like a man who had come to pay a courtesy call on his fiancée, she thought, her teeth sinking worriedly into her lower lip.

"Oh dear, it does look as if he is in a pucker," Mrs.

Beachton said, shifting her weight from one foot to another. "Do you think he has learned I am the one who started those silly stories?"

"I am sure I do not know," Pip said, dropping the edge of the drapes as she turned from the window. "But I do agree he doesn't look at all pleased."

"Perhaps you could explain it to him," Mrs. Beachton suggested, raising imploring eyes to Pip's face. "You are so clever with words, and I would only make a hash of it if I were to try."

Pip, who had been wondering how she could tactfully request to meet privately with Alex, seized upon her aunt's hesitant request. "Yes, it might be best if I see him alone," she said with a wise nod. "He is eventempered as a rule, but no man can like having his name dragged through the mud, regardless of the cause."

"You need not make your explanations to me." Mrs. Beachton raised both her hands, more than willing to abdicate responsibility to Pip. "His lordship is your fiancé, and an engaged couple are permitted some time alone. Only mind you don't linger in the study overly long. We wouldn't wish the servants to gossip." This last part was added with an admonishing frown lest her niece think her lax in her duties as duenna.

"I shall be but a few minutes," Pip promised, her heart pounding in dread of the coming confrontation. "Shall we say twenty?"

"Fifteen," her aunt bargained, not wishing to be thought a slackard in such things.

"Very well," Pip capitulated with a sigh. "Now if you will excuse me, I suppose I really should change. I would not wish his lordship to catch me like this." And she glanced down at her wrinkled gown.

"I shall have the butler bring him tea," Mrs. Beachton promised, taking great comfort in the fact

Phillipa wanted to preen for her fiancé. Perhaps this might all work out after all, she thought, quietly closing the door behind her. Heaven only knew it could not get any worse.

Thirteen

It seemed as if he'd spent half his life in this drawing room waiting for Pip, Alex mused, studying the familiar blue and white flocked wallpaper with a sad smile. He'd grown almost as comfortable here as he was in his own rooms at home. More so, in fact, because with Pip he had never felt more at home in his life. He would be sad to see the last of it.

The thought had him turning from the wall with a sigh. Forsaking the tea tray the butler had provided, he made his way to the cherry sideboard for the decanter of brandy he had spied on an earlier visit. After pouring himself a generous swallow, he downed it in a single gulp and was considering a second serving when common sense stayed his hand. The next few minutes would be difficult enough without getting bosky, he lectured himself, returning the glass stopper to the decanter. As in a battle, he would need all his wits about him if he hoped to survive.

How the deuce had he made such a muddle of things, he wondered with a heavy sigh. His only intention had been to guard Pip's reputation, and he had failed miserably to do that. According to Marcus, the story they had overheard was indeed the talk of London, and the worst of all was that even Marcus himself seemed to think it held a kernel of truth.

"You wouldn't be the first man who wished to line

his pockets under such circumstances," the earl had said with a shrug. "Not exactly sporting, but not precisely dishonorable either. Besides, what does it matter? Whether or not you and Miss Lambert attend the ball, the talk will still continue. It is the way of our world, Alex, and there is nothing you can do that will alter that."

But it *did* matter—to him, at least—and it filled him with fury that he was helpless to protect Pip from the malicious tattle. He'd forced her into becoming his fiancée to save her, but instead he had exposed her to even more unsavory gossip. He'd lain awake most of last night wrestling with that, and in the dim light of early morning he had come to the most painful conclusion of his life. He would have to let her go.

Even now the thought of never seeing Pip again was like an enemy's saber thrust through his heart. He loved her, he admitted morosely. He loved her more than he thought it possible to love another living person, and he would let her go without lifting a finger to stop her.

The door opened behind him, and he heard the faint rustle of silk as it was closed again. He closed his eyes, briefly seeking courage in prayer, and then turned to face her, his features immobile with control.

"Thank you for seeing me on such short notice," he said with the cool dispassion one might show a stranger. "I did not know if you would be at home."

"I–I was due at Belle's for tea, but I had a headache," Pip stammered, her heart growing heavy at the stiff way he held himself. He had to be furious with her, she thought unhappily, and she really could not blame him. Her childish refusal to accept his word was unforgivable.

"I am sorry to hear that," Alex said, noting with a sinking stomach that she did look rather done in. Her green eyes were closer to gray, and the lively animation that usually graced her countenance was quite missing.

So much for his fine words about taking care of her, he thought with another flash of bitterness.

Pip saw the bitterness in his deep blue eyes and turned away, biting her lips to hold back a cry of pain. While hastily donning her clothes, she had rehearsed what she would say to him, weighing each word for its possible effect. Now those same words seemed artifice of the worst sort, and she knew only the truth would do. Drawing a deep breath, she turned to face him.

"Alex, I am sorry."

He gave her a blank look. "For what?" he asked, feeling more than a little confused. He'd been about to begin his carefully planned speech, and found her interruption distracting.

"For doubting you." Pip was determined not to be put off by his unwelcoming attitude. "You are a gentleman, and I know you would never lie to me. I know now that you didn't send your valet to place that bet, and I am sorry for thinking otherwise."

The bet, he realized dully—she was talking about the damned bet! "That is all right," he said in a heavy tone. "I suppose I do not blame you for doubting my integrity. In the brief time we have been acquainted, I've done little to give you a good opinion of me."

"Nonetheless I was wrong not to even listen to you," Pip continued doggedly, wishing he would drop his icy facade and rail at her. Even having him fly into one of his high rages was preferable to the cool indifference he was now displaying.

"Perhaps." He was willing to concede that much at least, remembering his pain as she had turned her back and walked away. Knowing she now believed his innocence was small consolation, and he clung to the knowledge that she did not think him totally lacking in honor. "Phillipa, there is something I need to tell you—"

"I would also like to apologize for the hateful things I said." Pip heard Alex's quiet words, but she had the bit between her teeth and was unwilling to stop until satisfied she had made amends.

"To imply you would sell yourself was monstrously unfair of me, and I shall never forgive myself for saying it. It is my wretched temper, you see. I was so angry I wanted to hurt you as I had been hurt, and I applied the knife where I knew it would cut the deepest. Can—can you ever forgive me?" She peeked up at him from beneath her lowered lashes, searching his face for any sign of emotion. There was none.

Seeing his proud Phillipa humbling herself was almost more than Alex could bear. He wanted to gather her up in his arms and kiss her until her words of contrition were sighs of delight, but he knew he did not dare. Still, he was unable to resist touching her in some small way, and so he raised his hand, laying a gentle finger against her trembling lips.

"No more," he said softly, his eyes roaming over her face as if committing each feature to memory. "You are forgiven for everything. I only hope you can also find it in your heart to forgive me."

"Forgive you? For what?" Now it was Pip who was confused, her eyes wide with distress as she searched his face for some clue of what he was saying.

"For forcing you into an engagement you did not want," Alex said simply. "For trying to make you my wife when you insisted you wanted no part of marriage. For dragging you into this blasted bet in the first place. For so many things, my dear, I scarce know where to start. Only know that I am sorry, so very sorry that I failed in the one thing I wanted to do above all others, and that is to protect you."

"But you *did* protect me," Pip protested, blinking back tears that suddenly threatened. "You are not responsible for that silly story about your valet. Aunt told me—"

"I failed, Pip." He shook his head at her, refusing to accept the small sop she offered to his pride. "I am intelligent enough to know when the world is sniggering behind its hand at me, and I really do not mind so much for myself. But for you—I mind very much for you. That is why I have decided we must end our engagement. It is the only way."

If Pip had thought last night was the greatest pain she could bear, she soon learned she was wrong. Even then, when she was raging at him and saying things she now blushed to recall, she had clung to the knowledge that they would still be together. Beneath her anger and her pain her love had remained her anchor, and now . . . She drew a trembling breath.

"But—but won't that just prove the gossips are right?" she asked, forcing herself to think calmly. "They are wagering you will break with me."

"After the prince's ball." Alex gave a jerky nod. "But if I announce the engagement is ended before the ball, then that should put an end to all the rumors."

"Or we could just not attend the ball at all, and still remain engaged," Pip suggested, swallowing her pride with a painful smile. "Wouldn't that prove just as efficacious?"

Her willingness to sacrifice herself to his pride made Alex even more determined to end this farce. He'd learned she was a lady of honor the day of the riot at Mayfields, but he could no longer allow her to pay for his crimes. Pushing aside his own feelings, he reached out to take her hand in his.

"From the start you have argued that you have no wish to marry me," he said, his thumb brushing over the back of her hand in gentle circles. "You all but begged me to reconsider my foolish actions, but I was so certain I knew what was right I would not listen to you. I was everything you named me: overbearing, arrogant, high-handed." His lips twisted in a rueful smile. "You were right to call me a tyrant, my sweet, for I see now that is what I was. That is why I want you to follow my lead in this. I am the one who put us in this hellish mess. Let me be the one to get us out."

Hellish mess. Pip felt as if she had been slapped across the face. Was that how he felt about their engagement? she wondered, staring blindly at the head bent over her hand. Her other hand came up as if to stroke back the thick black hair that had tumbled across his forehead, but just as she would have touched him, the hand dropped lifelessly to her side. "I suppose you are right, your lordship," she said, her voice dull. "Perhaps it would be best if we put an end to it."

Her words drove the knife deeper into Alex's heart. "Good, good," he said, his eyes briefly touching hers as he raised his head. "I shall send the notice 'round to the papers. For appearance's sake, it must look as if it is you who has thrown me over. I fear you may be labeled a jilt, Miss Lambert."

She managed a smile to match the one he gave her. "I have been called worse," she assured him in a tone that was almost light. "Shall . . . shall I see you again, your lordship?"

"It would probably be best if we did not—for now, at least," he added, forcing himself to his feet before he disgraced himself by falling at her feet and begging her for another chance. "I shall be returning for Parliament next year, however, and hope I may look to you to keep my nose to the grindstone. I am a dreadful laggard, you know."

"You may count upon me, Lord St. Ives," Pip said, feeling like a fool for exchanging inanities with him when she longed to be pleading with him to stay. "You must know I cannot abide sloth in a politician, especially in a—"

". . . Tory," he finished for her, his eyes suspiciously bright. He gave her a regal bow. "Goodbye, Phillipa. I shall never forget you."

"Alex—wait." Her voice stopped him just as he reached the door.

"Yes?" He did not turn around, his fingers clutching the doorknob with desperate strength.

"Your ring." She had tugged the glittering ring from her finger and was holding it in her palm. "You have forgotten it."

He did turn then, and the pained look in his eyes made her heart jolt to a halt. "Keep it," he said in a voice that was almost ragged with emotion. "I shall not be needing it again."

"But—"

He let go of the doorknob and was in front of her in the space of a heartbeat. He took her hand and slid the ring back onto her finger. "Keep it," he insisted, using his hold on her hand to pull her against his chest. His other arm stole around her waist, drawing her into an ardent embrace. He stared down at her face with glittering eyes moments before he took her mouth in a kiss unlike any he had ever given her. It was hard, and passionate, and full of a desperation she could almost taste.

Her mouth parted in response, but he was already pushing her away. She stared up at him in shock, unable to say anything. He touched her cheek with a hand that was almost as unsteady as her own, and then he was gone, the door slamming shut behind him.

The news that Phillipa had ended her engagement to Viscount St. Ives hit London with the impact of a bomb. Once again, Pip found her small home on Wilton Place besieged with callers. Pretending she wasn't at home or even refusing her callers entirely only seemed to add fuel to the fire. In the hope of avoiding an out-and-out riot, she finally admitted the demanding creatures into her drawing room. It was even worse than the first time, she thought, enduring her guests' malicious speculation with a stoic silence. At least then she had had the security of knowing Alex stood solidly behind her. Now she was alone, more alone than she had ever been in her life.

Her aunt had taken the news of the broken engagement by falling into a spell of the vapors, sobbing that she had destroyed her dearest darling's one hope of happiness, and would not be consoled. Pip was strongly tempted to confide her woes in Belle, but her notes to her friend had gone unanswered. She was beginning to think Belle was avoiding her when her friend appeared with the second wave of callers.

"I am glad you finally came to your senses, my dear," one of her aunt's friends confided with a smug nod. "The lad is not all he should be, and that's the sad truth of it. But then, there never has been a St. Ives who has ever amounted to anything," she nodded with an unpleasant cackle.

That brought Pip's head snapping up, her eyes sparkling with anger as they focused on the woman's lined face. "Alex served with distinction when he was in the army," she informed the caller in haughty tones. "He was even mentioned by name in one of Wellington's dispatches."

"Pooh, what is there to soldiering?" The woman rolled her shoulders and reached for another bun. "Killing and shooting—how difficult can it be?"

"Difficult enough so that your son never rose above the captaincy you bought him," Pip shot back, offending the lady enough so that she and three of her party soon departed in a high dudgeon. But if she thought Mrs. Perchley's departure would end the attacks on Alex, she was soon disappointed as another lady picked up the cudgels.

"It is very good of you, Miss Lambert, to defend the viscount after the horrid way he has used you," the woman, a Miss Crowell, said with a buttery smile. "It is obvious that he is a villain, and this stunt has put him well beyond the pale."

"Yes, and I must say I can think of no one who deserves society's censure more," Belle said, speaking for the first time. "I have said from the onset that St. Ives deserves to be punished, and after tonight, he will be."

"What do you mean?" Pip gave Belle a puzzled look, stunned by the malice in her voice.

"Oh, nothing." Belle hid a catlike smile behind her teacup. "I was but making conversation."

"No." Pip shook her head. "I would know what you meant, Belle. How shall Alex be punished?"

Belle's amber eyes narrowed as she studied her friend's strained face. "Why, only that tonight his lordship will finally receive the set-down he so richly deserves," she said silkily, aware she was risking her friendship with Pip. It was a calculated gamble on her part, but if she was right and Pip did love the viscount, then she was determined to do all that she could to heal the breach between them.

Pip's brows gathered in a frown as she pondered Belle's remark. She would have thought that after the announcement appeared in the papers, Alex would have beat a hasty retreat to the country until the gossip died down. That is what she would have done had she any place to flee to, she admitted, even though it was probably a cowardly thing to do. Cowardly—the word halted her musings, and her eyes sprang open in a horrified understanding.

"He is going to Carlton House?" she gasped, her face paling as she realized it was precisely the sort of thing Alex would do. He would rather face society's ridicule than retreat to safety, and the thought of him subjecting himself to such humiliation was enough to make her forget her own pain.

"Yes. That wretch Colford was round to see me this morning, and he let it slip that St. Ives means to attend the prince's ball alone," Belle said, the very picture of cool disdain. "Evidently he thinks to brazen his way through the evening in his usual high-handed fashion, using his title and fortune as a shield."

"Alex is nothing like that!" For the first time in their

friendship Pip could see why the earl had called Belle The Golden Icicle. "That isn't why he's going to Carlton House!"

"Well, what other reason can there be?" Belle gave a disbelieving laugh. "It is obvious he is going merely to thumb his nose at society, and to show how little your engagement meant to him. A gentleman—"

"Alex is every inch a gentleman—and if he is going to the ball, it is because he refuses to run like a coward!" Pip was on her feet and glaring at Belle in fury.

"Well, upon my word, Miss Lambert, there is no need for you to shriek at Miss Portham," Miss Crowell declared, her sharp nose twitching with displeasure. "She is only speaking the truth. Besides, I fail to see why you are becoming so emotional. One would almost think you to be in love with the man, the way you leap so passionately to his defense."

"I *am* in love with Alex!" Pip exclaimed—and then clapped her hand over her mouth, sinking to her chair as she realized what she had said.

Her confession threw the drawing room into chaos. Her visitors began snatching up their reticules and shawls, eager to be gone so that they might be the first to spread the news to their dearest friends and worst enemies. Within minutes the room was emptied, leaving Pip alone to face Belle.

"Well, you certainly know how to make an announcement," Belle commented, calmly helping herself to a second cup of tea. "Thank heavens you were only saying that to be rid of them."

"No, I *do* love Alex," Pip insisted, annoyed that Belle should think her capable of such duplicity.

Belle gave a light laugh. "Oh come, Pip, we both know that is simply not so. From the moment your engagement was announced, you have done nothing but insist that you did not wish to marry his lordship. You have pouted, and railed, and schemed to get out of this engagement, and now you are out of it. Let it go. Besides, you seem to have forgotten your credo: Better the shroud than the veil, remember?"

Pip was on her feet again, pacing the room as if she could somehow outrun her own turbulent thoughts. "Perhaps I was wrong," she said, her mind in a whirlwind of confusion. "Alex is nothing like my father; I see that now. Perhaps marriage with him would not be so bad after all."

"Well, it is all a moot point now, isn't it?" Belle pointed out with a cool smile. "You have publicly rejected him, and all of the *ton* knows it. And tonight, when he appears at the ball without you, he faces being laughed out of London. Do you really think he can ever forgive you for that?"

"The ball!" Pip whirled around, all of her turmoil vanishing as she knew instinctively what she must do. "What time does it begin?"

"The dinner is at ten o'clock, with dancing to follow." Belle had already committed the information to memory, having read of it in the gazette.

"I must send Alex a note at once," Pip decided, dashing to the small desk in the corner of the room. "I shall write and tell him—"

"Tell him what? That you have no pride whatsoever?" Belle interrupted in a disdainful tone. "Besides, if what you are saying is so and his lordship means to face society as some sort of penance, what makes you think he will take you with him? He will doubtlessly forbid you to attend."

Pip's face paled, as she could easily imagine Alex doing just such a thing. "But I cannot allow him to do this," she said, fighting back the tears that threatened so easily these days. "You do not know him as I do, Belle, else you would know what a wonderful thing he is doing. He is so very proud. It will destroy him to know society is laughing at him!"

Belle had to bite her lip to keep from dashing to Pip's side—as all her instincts urged her to do. Drawing on her early years when she'd had to disguise her every thought and emotion, she managed to drag up a cool smile. "I still say it is no less than the scoundrel deserves," she said with calculated indifference. "But if you are determined to throw yourself on the funeral pyre with him, I see no difficulty. You still have your invitation, do you not?"

"Yes." Pip thought of the elegant embossed card she had already put away for her memory book.

"Well, there you are. Only present yourself at Carlton House and the card will grant you entry."

"Attend *alone?* Without a chaperone or escort?" Pip was shocked by such a suggestion.

Belle hid a smile. "It *is* a trifle unconventional," she admitted, praying she wasn't helping her dearest friend commit social suicide, "but hardly unheard of. Naturally, if you value convention above your precious Alex's tender feelings, I can understand your reluctance. Ah well, the Season is almost ended, and by next year this will all but be forgotten.

"Speaking of the Season ending, I was hoping to convince you and your dear aunt to visit me at Greenwood this summer. I thought—Pip, where are you going?"

"To begin my toilet for this evening," Pip replied, her eyes shining with a determined light as she started for the door. "I am sure you will forgive me if I do not see you to the door."

"Do you mean you are actually going to do it?" Belle sat up, her eyes wide with feigned dismay. "You are going to salvage St. Ives's pride at the risk of your own?"

"Yes," Pip announced calmly, "I am." And she closed the door behind her.

Belle's lips curved in a pleased smile. "Good," she said, pouring herself another cup of tea and planning what she would wear to the wedding.

* * *

Alex stood stiffly in the Receiving Room at Carlton House, his face aching with the effort of keeping his expression under control. He had been here less than half an hour, and it was taking all that was in him to keep from bolting for the door. This was worse than being in battle, he decided, trying not to flinch at the giggle from the pretty brunette who was standing at his left. In a battle one need only fear death or injury, and usually one was too busy to do even that. Here, however, he could feel every look, hear every whispered word and laugh, and it was slowly killing him.

It wasn't just the gossip, or the knowledge that he had brought this disaster down on his own head. He didn't give a bloody damn what these idiots thought, and he had never been one to back away from the consequences of his actions. No, what made this all so unendurable was the fact that once this evening was ended, he would never see Pip again. The thought was so painful that he had to clench his jaw to hold back a moan of anguish.

"Courage, your lordship." Marcus materialized at his side, his eyes soft with commiseration. "Prinny will soon be honoring us with his presence, and once this mob catches sight of his latest assault on fashion, they will forget all about you."

"That bad, is it?" Alex turned to his friend with a wry smile.

"Worse. The jacket he is wearing is in such extraordinary poor taste it will be all the crack within a week," Marcus assured him, his light words belied by the worry on his face. "How are you?"

Alex did not pretend to mistake his meaning. "Better than I have any right to be," he said quietly. "There have been few out and out insults, although I have heard enough innuendoes and double entendres to last me a lifetime."

"I still don't see why you didn't just say to hell with it and leave town," Marcus said with his usual bluntness. "This isn't the field of honor, you know, and no one would fault you for leaving."

"I would fault myself," Alex said, aware of a stir behind him. The prince must be making his appearance, he decided, but just as he was turning he heard the prince's majordomo call out in a loud voice, "Miss Phillipa Augusta Lambert."

At first Alex was certain he was hearing things, but when the buzz of conversation around him became an oppressive silence, he knew his ears had not played him false. As if in a dream, he swung slowly around, his eyes widening at the sight of Phillipa making her way through the crowd to his side.

She was wearing a gown of yellow silk, the pearls he had given her clasped around her neck. Her dark hair was swept up in a stylish coiffure, and he had never seen her looking lovelier. He was still drinking in her appearance when she paused in front of him.

"I am so sorry for keeping you waiting, your lordship," she said, offering him her hand with a repentant smile. "But the streets are positively thick with gawkers, and then that wretch at the door seemed disinclined to let me in. I had to threaten him with your infamous temper; I hope you do not mind?"

"Not at all," he managed, taking her hand and raising it to his lips. "You look beautiful."

She smiled in pleasure at his remark, and then turned to Marcus. "Your lordship." She dropped a graceful curtsey. "I trust you are well?"

"Quite well," Marcus replied, his eyes glowing with admiration. He knew what she had risked in coming as she had, and he only hoped St. Ives appreciated her sacrifice. Although if the stunned expression on his friend's face was any indication, he understood all too well what she had done—and why.

The crowd was closing in around them, and as if

from a distance Alex could hear their eager questions and Pip's calm reply.

"Oh, that was just some of Alex's old friends' idea of a prank!" she said with an indulgent laugh. "Of *course* we are still engaged. See?" And she held up her hand so that all might see the St. Ives diamond glittering on her finger.

The arrival of the prince provided a much-needed respite, and while the crowd was bowing to the regent, Alex grabbed Pip's hand and began dragging her toward the nearest door. It led out onto a small terrace. The moment they were out of doors he turned to her in confusion.

"What the devil are you doing here?" he demanded, his brows meeting in a scowl. "I would have thought you'd be halfway to the country if you had a whit of sense."

Pip's heart shattered at his angry words, an emotion that was quickly followed by pure fury. "You are not the only one who dislikes being thought a coward," she retorted, her chin coming up. "I have no intention of retreating to the country like some disgraced wife. If you know your duty, then so do I."

"But damn it all, what about your reputation?" Alex demanded, unable to believe she could have done anything so half-witted. "Do you know what you risked in coming here as you did? What if I weren't here, or if I had brought another woman? What would you have done then?"

Such possibilities hadn't even crossed Pip's mind, something she knew better than to admit. "I would have managed," she said through gritted teeth. "Now if you are finished ringing a peal over my head, it is time we were joining the others." She turned to go, but his grip on her arm stayed her.

"Phillipa—wait."

"What is it?" she asked, her heart hammering in awareness of his strong fingers on her bare arm.

"Thank you," he said softly, drawing her back against him. "I do not know why I am raging at you, when I ought to be on my knees thanking you. It is a very brave thing that you have done, and I want you to know how grateful I am. I would never have asked such a thing of you."

His words made her eyes close in pain. "I did not do it for your gratitude," she said with a bitter laugh, wishing the stones beneath her feet would crumble and drop her into oblivion.

"Then why did you do it?" Alex's arms tightened around her waist, holding her fast when she would have turned away. His heart was hammering with awareness as he studied her moonlit face. "Why, Pip?"

Lies, half-truths, and evasions burned on her tongue, but Pip could not bring herself to utter them. What did it matter if he knew? she wondered, her shoulders slumping with defeat. She had already blurted out her love to half of London, and the only wonder was that he hadn't already heard the juicy details. She sighed and raised her eyes to his face. "Because I could not bear for you to face disgrace alone," she said simply.

"Why?" Alex's hand trembled as he raised it to caress her face. He saw her answer in her eyes, but he longed to hear it from her lips.

"Because I love you."

His eyes closed as relief washed over him in a warm tide. "Thank God," he muttered hoarsely. "Thank God." And then his lips closed on hers in the sweetest of kisses.

"I love you," he whispered, his lips caressing hers. "God, Pip, I love you more than life itself!"

His urgently-whispered words filled Pip with a happiness that was so great it threatened to overwhelm her. She returned his kisses eagerly, losing herself in the wonder of a dream come true.

"Alex." His name was like a sigh on her lips as her

hands buried themselves in his thick hair. "Oh, my dearest love . . ."

They continued kissing, sharing whispered confessions between heated caresses. "I think I knew I loved you when you called me a fashionable fribble," he teased, his breath ragged as he struggled for control. "I was utterly furious, but at the same time I wanted to keep you in that room with me forever and never let you out."

"And I think I knew I loved you when you raged at me and called me a hoyden," Pip admitted, feeling greatly daring as she ran a finger down the length of his nose.

"What time was that, my love?" Alex caught her finger between his teeth and gave it a playful nip. "I have called you a hoyden any number of times."

"So you have," Pip agreed, her eyes twinkling. "In fact, I quite wonder why I should even contemplate marrying such an overbearing tyrant as you. Perhaps I should reconsid—"

He silenced her with another kiss. "Forget it, hoyden," he ordered in a voice that was not quite steady. "You are marrying me the moment I can arrange a special license, and that is final. Do you hear me?"

Pip snuggled against his chest. "I hear you, your lordship," she said with a happy sigh. "And after tonight I suppose we really *don't* have a choice. We are utterly compromised, and if you do not marry me, I shall have no choice but to call you out. And for your information, sir, I am a dead shot."

"I am already quaking in my boots." Alex smiled, then tipped her face up to hers. "I am serious, you know," he said, his eyes dark with love. "I do love you, and if you will not marry me then you might as well put a bullet through my heart now and be done with it. If I cannot have you as my wife, I am better off dead."

His confession brought tears to Pip's eye. "I feel the same," she told him, smiling through her tears. "I used to say 'better the shroud than the veil,' but I know now which I prefer. You need not fear I shall beg off, my darling; I will marry you whenever it pleases you."

They resumed their passionate kissing, and might have continued in this delightful pursuit forever had it not been for the sound of someone clearing his throat behind them. Alex raised his head first, his eyes widening at the sight of the man stepping from the shadows.

"Your Highness!"

Prince George regarded the embracing couple with amusement. "Ah, Lord St. Ives, Miss Lambert," he said with a rich chuckle. "We are delighted to learn that the rumors of your engagement ending are premature. However, we really must insist that you return to our dining room. It would not do for the guests to expire from hunger—and curiosity," he added, his light blue eyes shining with mischief.

"Your pardon, sir." Alex gave a hasty bow, aware of the burning desire to get Pip off to himself for some more kisses. "But I am afraid we must be leaving. I—"

"Oh, no you don't." The regent waggled a bejeweled finger at him. "I have a thousand quid on this, and I must insist that you stay for the waltzing. In fact, I think you should stay even longer. This shall be your engagement ball."

"That is very good of you, Your Highness," Alex tried again, only to be interrupted by the prince.

"Oh no, 'tis no trouble at all," he assured Alex with a beatific smile. "We shall be honored. Now I must go and inform my chef we shall be needing a cake. Five minutes, St. Ives. That is an order."

"Yes, Your Highness." Alex bowed again, smiling in gratitude. "Thank you."

"You are welcome." Prince George inclined his head regally. "Just mind you use them well." And he turned to make his way back to the massive dining room where his guests awaited. Ah, young love, he thought with a sentimental sigh, was there anything like it? He cast one last look at the embracing couple and smiled again. Maybe he would give the viscount *ten* minutes . . .

Avon Regency Romance

Kasey Michaels

THE CHAOTIC MISS CRISPINO
76300-1/$3.99 US/$4.99 Can

THE DUBIOUS MISS DALRYMPLE
89908-6/$2.95 US/$3.50 Can

THE HAUNTED MISS HAMPSHIRE
76301-X/$3.99 US/$4.99 Can

Loretta Chase

THE ENGLISH WITCH
70660-1/$2.95 US/$3.50 Can

ISABELLA
70597-4/$2.95 US/$3.95 Can

KNAVES' WAGER
71363-2/$3.95 US/$4.95 Can

THE SANDALWOOD PRINCESS
71455-8/$3.99 US/$4.99 Can

THE VISCOUNT VAGABOND
70836-1/$2.95 US/$3.50 Can

Jo Beverley

EMILY AND THE DARK ANGEL
71555-4/$3.99 US/$4.99 Can

THE STANFORTH SECRETS
71438-8/$3.99 US/$4.99 Can

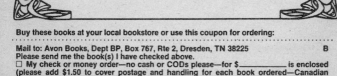

Avon Romantic Treasures

*Unforgettable, enthralling love stories,
sparkling with passion and adventure
from Romance's bestselling authors*

1 Out Of 5 Women Can't Read.

1 Out Of 5 Women Can't Read.

1 Out Of 5 Women Can't Read.

1 Xvz Xv 5 Xwywv Xvy'z Xvyz.

1 Out Of 5 Women Can't Read.

*As painful as it is to believe, it's true. And it's time we all did something to help. Coors has committed $40 million to fight illiteracy in America. We hope you'll join our efforts by volunteering your time. Giving just a few hours a week to your local literacy center can help teach a woman to read. For more information on literacy volunteering, call **1-800-626-4601**.*

LITERACY. PASS IT ON.